SEASON ONE: EPISODE FOUR

SUNSET CHRONICLES

BLINDED BY LIGHT

PAUL STEPHENSON

HOLLOW STONE

For Writers United, the best accidental writing community ever

Note for readers

The Sunset Chronicles is a sci-fi serial. Think of it like a series, much like you'd get on your favourite tv streaming service. There are seasons, split up into episodes (five per season). Each episode is designed to be read in roughly two hours, though fast readers may blast through them even quicker, and those who like to really get stuck into the story may take longer. They're intended to be thrilling and exciting, and are released regularly each month so that you can keep up with the story even if you have a hectic schedule. And who doesn't, these days? It's perfect for if you want to slip some space horror into your lunch break, or if you want to binge it of an evening.

If you've come to this book first, please check out episode one, *Last Light*, which is available in print and ebook.

Also, although *The Sunset Chronicles* is a story that stretches from the ice moon of Europa to every corner of the globe, its author remains English. As such, international readers should note that spellings are of the UK variation of English, so if you see a typo, it must be because of that.

If you're in the UK and you see a typo, it must be your imagination.

Chapter One

Lois staggered backward, bumping into a pedestrian who'd joined in gawking at the blood-splattered sight laid out in the middle of a busy Atlanta street.

Neil. Poor, nervous Neil.

'Excuse me, miss?'

It took Lois a moment to realise the police officer, a tall black man with grey flecks in his beard, was talking to her.

'Uh, yes?'

'Did you know this man?'

'I...' She looked around. Uniformed officers moved people back, clearing the scene. Flashing lights washed over them, robbing Lois of her equilibrium. What the hell had happened? She looked back at the man. He stared at her, pad in hand. 'Yes. He's my secretary.'

'Sunset?'

She nodded.

'Okay, would you mind coming with me?'

'What happened to him?'

'That's what we're trying to find out, miss.'

Before Lois could react, hands guided her into a police pod, the man with the salt and pepper beard leaving her behind. He whispered something to another officer, a woman with close-cropped red hair. Plainclothes like him. She nodded her agreement to whatever he was saying and climbed in after Lois. They sat opposite each other.

Before Lois could say anything, the pod moved away. 'Wait,' she said. 'Where are we going?'

'The station,' the woman replied, coolly.

'What for?'

'We need to ask you some questions about your colleague.'

Lois sat back, trying to compose herself, a hard task given the jackhammering in her chest.

Neil was dead. Killed in brutal fashion, in public. Was it coincidence the murder happened right on her path home? He'd left work long before her, but his body hadn't been there long. The scene was fresh. If it'd happened after he'd left, they'd have cleared it already. Had someone waited for her to leave and killed him to frame her?

Eyes covered every inch of Atlanta, roving cameras which blanketed the city with security. They'd be able to trace her from the moment she'd left Sunset, and he was already dead when she came to the intersection. The police had been on the scene already. Pretty hard to frame her. Or so she hoped.

No, the more likely scenario was even worse. He'd been waiting for her, and they'd killed him before he could speak to her.

But speak about what?

The pod ride was brief. At the station, the redhead led Lois through a side entrance. The woman made no move to speak, and Lois buried the million and one questions she had. No point giving anything away.

They walked through the main pen, empty save for a few drunk executives sleeping off their expensed indulgences. Nobody looked up at her, and she wasn't processed. Nobody took so much as a wrist scan. Thank heavens for small mercies.

Most of the station fell into two camps: cops and mysterious, black clad soldiers. Sunset's security forces. You could walk into any police station in America and find a few of them stationed as local liaisons. But she'd never seen so many in one place together. The effect was jarring, and when a few of them looked over to her, her stomach dropped. Had one of them slit Sardy's throat? Or Neil's?

The woman walked her to an interrogation room and pointed at the chair. 'Wait here. Someone will be in to see you soon.'

The door closed, leaving Lois under the harsh glare of the interrogation room lighting. She'd been on the other side of this table enough over the years to know that how she conducted herself in the next few hours was vital. If there was even a hint of suspicion on her, she could only confirm it. She had to play this just so—a woman who'd found her assistant dead in the street and had no idea what happened to him. Who might be in shock. Her instincts—to shut up shop, refuse to answer questions—they'd see her inside a cell. She was still undercover; she couldn't be an Interpol agent to these people.

An hour passed before the door opened again. The woman came back in, looking at her pad, followed by the older black man with the salt and pepper beard.

'Sorry to keep you waiting,' the man said. They both took their seats opposite. 'I'm Detective Jones, this is Detective Stone.'

'Can you please tell me what's going on?' Lois replied.

'You said the man in the street was your secretary?'

'Yes.'

'How long has he worked for you?'

'A few days. I started working at Sunset this week.'

'And Neil got assigned as your secretary?'

'Yes.'

'Who by?'

'Sorry?'

'Who assigned you to Neil? Or him to you?'

'I don't know what that's got to do with anything.'

The two cops looked at each other, and the woman gave a nod.

Detective Stone pulled up her pad and tapped the screen. An image came up. Dan Sardy, smiling. A candid photo taken at some party, taken from his social feed no doubt. Shit, were there pictures of the two of them together on their feeds? She doubted it.

'Do you recognise this man?' Jones asked.

Lois leaned forward and shook her head. 'No, I don't think so.'

'Murdered two weeks ago. In public, like Neil.'

'I'm sorry, no. I wasn't even in Atlanta.'

'Where were you?' the woman asked, revealing a northern accent Lois hadn't caught before. Boston, perhaps. A refugee escaped from the flooded east.

'My work takes me around the world. I've recently returned from a job in Canada.'

'You wouldn't mind if we checked that out?' Stone asked, leaning forward.

'Of course not.'

Stone got up and left, leaving Lois alone with Jones, who sat back, appraising Lois. Neither said anything. Jones stared at Lois, playing with something in his hands.

Stone came back in. 'Checks out,' she said, sounding half disappointed.

'Okay, Mrs Pertin,' Jones said, wearily. 'Thanks for your help. You're free to go.'

'Wait,' Lois said. 'I don't understand. Can you please tell me what's going on? Who is that man, and what does he have to do with Neil?'

'That man was Neil's former boss. Killed a few blocks away from Neil, along with a woman. Initial investigation chalked it up as a robbery, but his secretary turns up dead a few weeks later. I'd guess there's a common thread there. You're new to the company, so I'm sure there's no reason for you to worry, but if you see anything suspicious, you call the station.'

Lois sat, trying to process everything, giving nothing away to the detectives scrutinising every movement she made. Neil had told her, in his roundabout way, that he knew what Dan had been looking into, had worked out Lois might play for the same team, and that he could help her.

She'd been too damn stupid to spot it.

Someone hadn't. The smart money was on Burgess, no doubt watching their conversation, taking from it what Lois missed. Neil paid the price for her being too caught up in the contents of the rack pad.

She'd blown it.

'Are you saying my life could be in danger?' she asked.

Jones shrugged. 'I doubt it, ma'am.'

As Jones and Stone led her out of the station, Lois mumbled her goodbyes, wanting desperately to sneak in a suggestion they look into the black-clad operatives watching proceedings. She declined the offer of a police escort home, although it might not have been the worst idea, and tried to get her bearings.

She looked at her wrist. Well past midnight. She'd not heard from Marisa, either. She could get in contact with Findlay, he could tell her if they'd made the glide okay. It was too late to be calling her parents.

The streets were cold and empty. The city had gone to bed, leaving Lois more exposed than she liked.

God damn it. If Sunset had bumped off Neil following her conversation with him, a dialogue so obtuse as to be impenetrable even to her, then their level of paranoia was sky high. She had to tread carefully.

Nothing she'd uncovered was bad enough to merit this kind of overreaction. Enough for a couple of execs to lose their jobs, but nothing a company the size of Sunset couldn't endure. Shit, they'd barely see a dent in their daily share price, so why risk such high-profile murders? A company the size of Sunset worked strictly on risk vs reward.

By the time she got home, her ankles ached. As promised, Findlay had tucked a tiny chip into the wood. Peeling off the chip behind her ear, she swapped it out, placing the one from today back in the old wooden frame, palming the one for tomorrow.

The house was silent, holding its breath for her return. She wanted to call out to her girls, but they weren't there. Easing her shoes off, she placed the chip on the living room table, lay down on her sofa, and went straight to sleep.

Chapter Two

'Good morning,' A disembodied voice said.

Judd opened his eyes with some difficulty. He was in a bed. Walker sat opposite in his wheelchair, staring at Judd with piercing eyes. He wasn't alone. Mrs Smith sat beside him, face as stern as the day before. Lan stood by the door looking frightened, hands behind her back.

'Morning,' Judd said, although it came out as more of a croak than words. He wasn't in the room they'd given him; this one was bigger, plusher. There were pictures on the walls, and the furniture was far less functional. 'What happened?'

'A good and interesting question, Judd,' Walker replied. 'What do you remember?'

'Um,' Judd said, trying to reassemble the events as they'd happened. 'There was, um, a fight?'

'Yes. You remember what happened at the end of the argument?'

The memory came back. Light swelling within him, a rush of energy. 'No.'

'I see. Well, it seems we have a problem with you, Judd.'

'What kind of problem?'

'You're a block,' Mrs Smith chimed in.

'A what?'

'You can suppress the gift in others,' she continued. If she was making any effort to conceal the disgust in her voice, she was doing a piss-poor job of it. 'You can block them, you can switch them off, almost, but you also do something more.'

'The light?'

'You remember?' Walker asked. 'The gifted in the cafeteria said you glowed, radiated light. And yet, the ordinary people working in the cafeteria saw nothing of the sort. They saw two people facing off against each other, and everyone in the cafeteria fell over. Apparently, it was quite funny, if you like that sort of thing.'

'I didn't find it funny,' Lan added.

'Quite,' Mrs Smith agreed. 'Several of our students and operatives are still in the hospital wing, while it seems Bertrand, the boy you fought, has been...' She looked away from him. 'Stripped of his gift.'

Lan looked at her shoes, shaking her head, while Walker's piercing glare never left Judd.

'We will have to see what happens there,' Walker said. 'Let's give the hospital wing the resources they need and some time, before we completely write him off.'

'I...' Judd offered, but couldn't manage anything else.

'Bertrand and his cohorts can be arrogant,' Walker said. 'Insufferable, even downright unpleasant, but what they tried to convey to you, Judd, was that while you might have seen your first day as a failure, you could still hear them, that all was not lost. I understand they used that lesson to say mean things to you, though the punishment exceeds the crime.'

Lan shook her head. If Walker was ready to forgive him, it was clear he still had a long way to go with her.

'I didn't mean...' he stammered. 'I don't know what...'

'Still,' Walker said, holding up his hand. 'It leaves us with something of a conundrum. You are special, Judd. You have a completely new gift, something we've never seen before. But you are also dangerous, and not in the ways we deal with every day. You're dangerous to us. In the years we've been out, people have tried to harm us. They resort to violence, because they cannot control without crude means. We have endured, because we have the upper hand. But you are everything the normal human population needs. You could be their greatest weapon. You can block us, you can get inside our heads, and worse, you can rob us of the gift.'

'I don't mean to.'

Mrs Smith chimed in; 'Wishing it doesn't make it less so.'

A silence fell over the four of them.

'Pardon me for asking, sir,' Judd said, trying to sit up in the bed, 'but should you be in here, with me? Isn't it a risk?'

Walker smiled. 'The fact you'd ask tells me no, I don't believe it is. You still have a gift, Judd. You share some of the same traits as some of our other students, but your gift is different. We can train you on how to control it, how to use it to the benefit of your own people. We can help you.'

'The other students won't like it,' Lan said, in a low voice.

'I understand, Lan,' Walker continued. 'They will have to adjust. Judd, you will find your time here difficult. I suspect you will struggle to make friends. People will not trust you, be fearful of you. The longer people are here, the more they appreciate their gifts, make it a defining part of who they are. They will see you as a threat to that.'

'Judd,' Mrs Smith interjected, leaning forward and placing a frail hand on his own. 'Do you believe you can control this ability of yours?'

Judd struggled to find the words. 'Until Mr Walker came along, I had repressed it my whole life. I don't understand how you knew I had it. Before yesterday, I had no problem keeping it in check. Now I know it's there... I don't know. I hope so?'

'I guess it'll have to do,' Mrs Smith said, leaning back in her chair.

'I suggest you get some rest,' Walker said. 'This is my apartment, so I would ask you not to go nosing around. There is a feed screen, if you so desire. Until we've figured out our next steps, I ask you not to leave this apartment. Lan will be by with some food later.'

Mrs Smith stood, taking Walker's chair. Lan opened the door, and without even a backward glance, the three of them left. The door closed, the locking mechanism clunking loudly.

He let out a sigh and stared at the door.

It was clear the only two people who wanted him here were the old couple. And as nice as this apartment was, it was a cell. Judd wasn't naïve. Walker saw him as a weapon. One with the potential to be deployed against his people. Why hadn't they whisked him off to some underground bunker to wither away and die? Why not kill him while he slept?

Judd would go through life as a pariah, hated and distrusted by both sides. The way Lan had looked at him, the anger in her eyes; and she was as close to a friend as he had here.

For the next few hours he lay on Walker's bed, mulling things over, asking himself questions to which he had no answers.

Lan entered, carrying a tray. Judd sat up in the bed and took it, noting the lack of eye contact. She tried to leave.

'You're pretty pissed at me, huh?' he called.

She stopped, facing the door. For a moment he thought she might head straight out, but she whirled round, fists balled by her side. 'What you did was monstrous.'

'Those guys weren't saying pleasant things about you, you know.'

'It's a good job you're here to stand up for me, eh? You terrify me, Judd. Every time I walk into this room, I wonder if you're going to lose your temper and wipe my brain. Those times you got sulky with me, how close did I come? When you blocked Mrs Smith, I got a nosebleed. Did you wipe something I haven't discovered yet?'

'I don't know!' Judd shouted back, but as he raised his voice Lan's face turned to absolute horror, and she stumbled out of the room.

'Lan, wait,' he called, but the door locked behind her.

Shit.

He sat back. He hit the remote embedded in the bed frame, bringing up a feed screen, pre-programmed with news feeds. Food riots in Moscow. War in Europe. The Minos reaching Europa. The upcoming presidential race. Bombings. Mar. War. Storms. Floods. The same endless cycle of depressing news.

It felt like humanity was clinging onto this world by its fingertips, wondering how things got this bad with no way to turn things around. He clicked off the feed, searching through the vid feeds for something to distract him. He tried the comedy feeds, but it was dross—the harsh sounds of the audience's canned laughter clashing with the angry thoughts buzzing around his head, mocking him for his stupidity.

He'd have to learn to control this, whatever this was. No matter what he did; if he stayed, if he ran, he had to learn how to use this cursed gift. And a small part of him had to admit that if Lan was ever going to listen to him again, he'd have to earn her trust back. She'd never look at him the way he looked at her, but she was as close to a friend as he had in this world. She may be the only one he ever had. If that was going to carry on, he'd have to convince her not to run out of the room screaming every time he spoke.

He didn't want blood on his hands, metaphorical or otherwise. He would have to learn to control this gift, to understand it. Or at least try.

Chapter Three

When her alarm chirped the next morning, Lois woke feeling every decision she'd made had come home to roost in one terrible moment. Most pressing of these was the choice to fall asleep in her clothes on her sofa. Everything ached, from her ankles on up, culminating in a cricked neck that caused her first word of the day to be a winced 'fuck.'

She stood, stretching out different parts of her body in sequence, trying to coax them back to life. Even her head felt fuzzy, broken. As she worked her arms and shoulders, memories of the night before came flooding back. Memories of Neil in the street, dead. Of a police interrogation.

Marisa.

There was still no word, no message from her wife to say she'd gotten to her father's safely. Lois's sleep had filled with fractured dreams of Marisa and the girls, of them out of reach, drifting away.

Checking her watch, it was late enough to pester Marisa. Calling up her wife's wrist ID, she dialled it, her heart-rate steadily increasing with each unanswered ring. Finally, it clicked.

'Hey, honey,' Marisa said, sounding flustered. Commotion sounded in the background, and a cry from one of the girls. 'We're okay, we're here. Sorry for not letting you know, but I didn't want to disturb you at work.'

'It's okay,' Lois replied, tears of relief welling up but not spilling. Not yet, anyway. 'It's okay. I wanted to call you last night, but I got back too late.'

'Everything okay?'

'It's fine,' she lied. 'I'm glad you're okay.'

'We're fine. The girls are playing up today. They're excited to see Grandpop.'

'Good,' Lois said. The tears flowing, she struggled to keep them out of her voice. She wanted to run to her girls and scoop them up. Run and never look back.

Soon.

'Well, don't worry about us. Call when you can though, yeah?'

'I will. I love you.'

'I love you, too.'

Lois blew a kiss down the phone, a childish affectation she didn't think she'd done to Marisa since they were first together. Her wife laughed, startled. She was crying, too, Lois realised.

Marisa ended the call, leaving Lois standing in yesterday's clothes, crying.

Half an hour later—showered, dressed, and newly composed—she was on the pod network, heading toward the gleaming spires of Sunset's headquarters. It was a carriage pod, which was strange. Must be busy this morning—they rarely sent these around to the nicer parts of town. If you lived in a certain bracket, you didn't expect to have to share with the average person. Lois and Marisa's place wasn't at the top end of the bracket, but it was close enough so Lois rarely had to share air with the rest of Atlanta's residents in the morning.

Lois planned out her strategy for the day as the city whizzed past and stopped, whizzed past and stopped. The first problem was whether to bring up what happened. Probably the prudent approach, since Sunset's security team almost certainly knew Lois was at the scene. They probably had the interrogation footage. She'd call Burgess, tell her everything, and go from there. Even ask for advice.

Once she'd done that, it was back to the rack pad, trying to get as much viewed as possible. There had to be something in there.

Two seats down, a man stared at her. It took Lois a while to notice, longer than it should have done, but once she'd clocked him, there was no escaping it. Short man, olive skin, buzz cut and thick jaw. If he was surveilling her, he was doing a piss-poor job of it. She lowered her gaze from his, trying not to blush under the ferocity of his gaze even as it burrowed into the side of her face.

Senses heightened, she reviewed the rest of the pod. Sunset workers, some looking put out at their travel arrangements for the morning, but others, too. Casually dressed, doing their utmost to avoid looking at her. It was an old cop trick, to see who wouldn't meet your gaze. Stare at someone and their senses would let them know, and they'd look up. Evolutionary defence mechanism, no doubt. But if nobody looked up as she scanned the pod, then something was wrong.

Shit.

Something was wrong. There were no more stops before Sunset, so no opportunity to duck out. She needed to get the hell out of there, but there were no exits, and the final approach into Sunset was on a rail suspended a hundred feet above the ground. Even if she could stop the pod, there was no way off.

They pulled in; the pod slowing as it approached the station. There was one stop for the whole Sunset headquarters, but it was huge. A platform a few hundred feet long, with escalators leading off to the various parts of the campus. Even though they were on a carriage pod, its length took up a fraction of the platform.

A platform full of black-clad security officers.

A murmur went through the pod as those simply turning up for work noticed the security detail, a frisson of excitement tinged with fear that their morning would be more exciting than usual.

Her fellow passengers looked around nervously, trying to work out who amongst them was about to get dragged off the platform to a fate unknown. The fear on some said they suspected it might be them.

As for Lois, she could either let them take her and see where the chips fell, or make a run for it. Given the fall, and that she was firmly on Sunset's turf, the latter sounded a lot like suicide. Neither held much appeal, but at least the former might have a modicum of dignity in it.

Her thoughts drifted back to Tijuana. She'd needed an army of Interpol special forces then; she might need the same again. Hopefully Findlay was somewhere nearby working on a plan. But could he be?

In the middle of the platform, directly in front of where Lois's carriage came to a stop, Burgess stood, a wide smile plastered across her face. Any tiny fragment of hope Lois may have had that this was for anyone but her evaporated.

The pods stopped; Lois's door opened. Lois stood, clutching her bag. She waited for the other passengers to disembark, making sure nobody else was in any danger. The buzz-cut man and his friends made no move to leave the pod, or to get her to leave.

Composing herself, she stepped onto the platform.

'Burgess,' she said, trying to keep her voice calm and even. 'Bit of an overreaction, isn't it?'

Burgess gave a hollow laugh. 'We wanted to make sure an agent of an institution as esteemed as Interpol receives the appropriate welcome.'

Lois wondered briefly whether to bluff her way out. There was no bluff big enough. There was one other route. 'Would this be a good time to tell you you're under arrest?'

'Let's discuss it inside, shall we?'

A fan of security goons escorted her into the main lobby. Without wanting to seem like she was looking around wildly, she looked around wildly. This was going to end badly. To her left, there was a tiny gap in the formation of her escort.

Without thinking, Lois darted to it, dropping hard to her knees and rolling away under the arms of a guard before leaping to her feet, sprinting for the door. To her surprise—and that of the guards—it worked, albeit at the cost of bolts of pain from her knees. She dashed at full pelt toward the doors, back out into the pod bay.

An arm extended from somewhere. Her face slammed into it; her legs went out from underneath. She crashed to the ground, skull hitting the marble floor hard, teeth knocking together so hard her mouth filled with blood.

Lois's world filled with confusion and noise. The guard who'd taken her down had done so out of reflex more than intent, sprawling to the ground himself and struggling to get up. The nearest other guard was metres away.

Scrabbling to her feet, Lois headed for the door once more, falling down and scrambling to get back up again. Someone, some kind, sweet someone, held the door open out of surprise, and she was out on the platform.

The pods had moved on, the track empty. The rail was a thick metal bar running along and out of the station, and crucially, away from her pursuers.

Jumping down into the trench, she ran.

At the far end of the platform, the trench gave way, so she ran along a metal bar suspended high above the ground. A steep hill rolled beside her to the city. Sunset's headquarters towered over the rest of the city, and this hill was the reason why.

Teetering on the edge of falling, she jumped over to the grass, ignoring the calls and cries behind her. She started down the hill, half running, half sliding on her arse. The root of a tree caught her ankle, and she went flying forward, downward momentum gathering with every inch. She hit the hill again and tumbled, no longer running or sliding but falling, hitting each patch of earth hard, clothes tearing, skin tearing, too, until she hit the bottom.

Sirens sounded in the distance. Forcing herself up, her arms gave way beneath her, and darkness washed over her.

Chapter Four

'What did you see?' Wyn asked.

'I don't know,' Barnes replied. 'A creature. Animal of some sort. Large, completely white. Whiter than the ice, but with, like, red streaked down its front. I don't know. It fucking freaked me out.'

'Did it attack you?' Zoe asked, shining a torch into Barnes's eyes.

'Cut that shit out, will you, Zo?' Barnes replied, holding his hand up. 'No, it didn't attack me. I...' He sighed. 'I panicked. Turned and ran into one of the support struts.'

Sniggers broke out amongst the rest of them, except Wyn, who scanned the horizon, looking for movement.

'Yeah, okay,' Barnes said. 'Laugh it up. But we're not alone here, I swear to God.'

'We believe you,' Captain Davis said. 'But we don't know what it was. Could be you heard what Wyn said and your mind played tricks on you.'

'Heard Wyn?' Barnes said. 'Wait, you've seen something too?'

'You didn't hear?' Zoe asked.

'Comms has been playing up since you left,' Barnes said. 'I didn't hear a thing. That's why I came outside, I was going stir crazy in the quiet.'

Captain Davis stared out across the expanse of ice. 'Miles. You picking up life forms out here on the ice?'

'Nothing currently, Captain.'

'Technically, we've already met life,' Zoe said. 'This red stuff? Definitely alive. I've done compositional analysis of both the substances we've found, and the bright red stuff is, well, algae.'

'Algae?'

'Not dissimilar to what we'd find on Earth. It's got a radiation count much higher than life on earth, but stored at a cellular level. It's not emitting radiation. My guess is it thrives on the radiation from the magnetotail.'

'Is it the stuff we're here for?' the Captain asked.

'Yes and no,' Zoe replied, getting animated. 'The second compound we've found—the darker red which cracks and releases a gas on contact—shares properties with The Mar. I mean, eerily so. That's what the probe found, and sent us, which is weird, since there's a lot less of it than the algae, and there's no hint of the algae in the data the probe sent. But they're definitely linked. I need to run a lot more analysis, but I'm guessing we'll find the key to curing The Mar in the algae, not the other substance.'

'What is the other stuff?' Wyn asked.

'Beats me. I'm still trying to understand it. The steam is highly radioactive.'

'Let's get Barnes back inside,' Captain Davis said. 'We'll fix his helmet, make sure he's not done himself too much of a mischief. But we're on a tight clock—we need to get back to the others and under the ice before the magnetotail crests the horizon.'

Barnes went through the decontamination showers, followed by the others. Once inside, Miles stabilised the atmosphere and

Zoe and Barnes both took their helmets off. Wyn took her own off, too, revelling in the ability to breathe normally.

Hamza stood in his full suit, awkwardly watching the others.

'What?' Wyn said, placing her helmet on a table.

'It's just... Alien mould.'

'Algae.'

'Whatever. And creatures running around on the ice. Don't you think we should get the fuck off this rock as soon as humanly possible?'

'I hear that,' Wyn said.

Hamza sighed and took his helmet off, setting it aside. Wyn clasped his shoulder and gave him a sympathetic smile.

It didn't take Zoe long to patch Barnes up. He sported a fetching white bandage over one eye, where he'd crashed into the pillar. While they waited, Wyn printed some food for the rest of them, figuring it would be their last shot at something not entirely liquid for the rest of the day, at least.

Everyone looked exhausted. Zoe frowned at her pad. The others picked at their food. The reclaimed carbon offerings on the Andy were even worse than on the Minos. At least there they had condiments and flavourings to disguise the taste of bugs, but Wyn couldn't even tell what meal this was. It didn't even look like food.

She pushed some around her plate with her fork and contemplated ejecting the whole food printer into space.

Zoe leapt up, pad in hand. 'It's monster poop!' she exclaimed.

Wyn looked back at her plate and pushed it away.

'Sorry, what?' Captain Davis asked.

'It's...' she looked up and saw the round of confused faces. 'Sorry. So, we've got two substances, right? The algae, and a second substance. Both contain organic matter. I've been trying to determine the second substance based on the fact its interaction is with the algae. Like, one is a by-product of the other, right?'

She stood, pacing, talking more to herself than the rest of them.

'Except, how can that be, right? There would need to be a third party to the exchange, some kind of catalyst for the transformation. And this second substance is organic, but it's not an organism. It's not, itself, alive. So, I've been examining the algae, wondering if there's some kind of parasite within the molecular level of the algae, making the transformation. I mean, it would make sense, because The Mar's a parasite, too.'

'Zoe,' the Captain said. 'Slow down, okay?'

'Sorry. But if we have completely different organisms on the ice, living beings, they must eat something. Every animal needs to feed. So, what are they eating?'

'Algae!' Barnes shouted, his own enthusiasm matching the biologist's. 'Of course!'

'Sorry,' the Captain said, 'the rest of us are still lost here.'

'So,' Zoe continued. 'You've got an unknown animal which lives on the surface. What does it eat?'

'Algae,' Barnes replied.

'And what happens to the algae?'

'It becomes waste.'

'Monster poop,' Wyn said, finally catching on.

'Exactly!' Zoe said. 'We're seeing a symbiotic relationship between two organisms, perfectly in balance with each other. The creatures eat the algae, and they produce a waste product which in turns becomes fertiliser for the algae.'

'What about degradation?' Barnes asked. 'Food is energy. So there must be a degradation of the process with each cycle? Entropy always wins.'

'True,' Zoe said, frowning at her pad.

'Anyone else following this?' Hamza said, under his breath.

Wyn shrugged.

'The magnetotail!' Zoe shouted, ignoring Hamza. 'When the moon crosses into the threshold of the magnetotail, radiation floods the surface. Somehow, the radiation is the source of energy which becomes food for these creatures.'

'So, they're radioactive monsters?' Wyn asked.

Zoe ignored her. 'Obviously, the algae evolved to use it as a source of energy. The radiation supercharges the algae, and these animals, whatever they are, they get the nourishment they need from it.'

'It's genius,' Barnes said, staring at Zoe's pad with a grin.

'Okay, how does it help us?' the Captain asked.

Zoe looked stumped for a second. 'I don't know, but at least we have some idea what it is we're dealing with. It should help me understand the properties of The Mar they have in common, and how we can use these compounds to combat the parasite back on Earth. If I could get my hands on one of the creatures...'

Captain Davis scoffed. 'Not on your life, Zoe.'

'I'm not sure bringing one on board would be a good idea,' Wyn said.

'Yeah,' Barnes said. 'We've already got Miles, I'm not sure we need another pet.'

'I'm not a pet, Doctor,' Miles interjected.

'The key is understanding this relationship,' Zoe said. 'If it means capturing one of these animals...'

'Hang on,' Wyn said. 'We've not even seen them yet. They might be vicious killers.'

'Their main food is algae,' Zoe said. 'Chances are they're harmless.'

'Didn't look harmless to me,' Barnes muttered.

The Captain held his hands up. 'We've only got a few hours until the magnetotail boils us in our suits, so I'd say this is a moot point. We don't have an animal to examine, and we're not going to waste time trying to find one.'

Zoe opened her mouth to protest, but an arched eyebrow was enough to persuade her otherwise. The Captain continued.

'Let's get back to the others. Get under the ice. We can work out what the plan is from there.'

They fell silent. A smile spread across Zoe's face. 'Think about it,' she said. 'Intelligent life. The biggest question humanity has ever had, and we might be about to find out the answer. It's kind of...'

A loud boom echoed through the Andy, cutting her off. The lights dimmed, flickered, and came back on.

Another loud boom, and the lights cut out entirely for a second. The surrounding metalwork groaned.

'Miles?' Captain Davis called out. 'What the fuck is going on?'

'It appears...' Miles replied, his voice as calm and implacable as ever. Another loud boom interrupted him, the sound compounded by creaking metal. 'It appears Zoe's creatures wish to investigate us, too.'

'Suit up, everyone,' Captain Davis shouted.

'Told you,' Hamza muttered, reaching for his helmet. 'Should never have taken the fucking thing off.'

'Miles, pull up external feed,' Wyn said, fastening her own helmet.

A small vid display lit up on the far wall of the cargo bay, revealing a grainy view of one of the support struts, and the long curve of one of the boosters. Below it, nothing but white ice.

Something careened in from the corner of the screen, charging at the strut at high speed. It hit the strut and bounced off, out of sight, tumbling back out of view. They felt the impact a split second later. Hamza fell to the ground.

'Miles, play back at half speed,' Wyn said.

The crew stared at the screen as it wound back, and Miles froze the picture on the creature as it was about to hit the strut.

It was unlike anything Wyn had ever seen. The image was black and white, but you could see how pale the creature was. It was huge, with a rotund body and a head like the end of a hammer. Coming from the body was a blur that could be fins, or claws.

They couldn't see the face, but Wyn almost didn't want to. The rest was horrifying enough.

'What the fuck?' Barnes said.

'You still want to take one of those home, Zo?' Hamza said.

Wyn turned to the Captain. 'What the fuck do we do?' she asked. 'We've got no weapons, nothing to defend ourselves with.'

'You think one of those things could take out one of the support struts?' Barnes asked.

'Maybe,' Hamza said.

'Zoe,' the Captain said. 'If we take off and head back to the Minos, is there any way the good people at Sunset could get what they need from the samples we already have?'

'None.'

'And half the crew are at the fissure,' Barnes added.

'We need to repel this... whatever the fuck it is. Do we have anything on board we can use as a weapon?'

'I can try to rustle something up,' Hamza said.

'Do it.'

'What about the boosters?' Wyn said. 'We're already planning on short bursts to clear out the build-up of algae. I could fire them, clear out whatever is underneath us. If nothing else, it might scare them away.'

'No,' the Captain said. 'You'd be burning fuel we need.'

'Captain,' Wyn insisted. 'We've got plenty of fuel.'

'No,' Captain Davis insisted.

'Captain!'

He fixed her with a hard stare, broken by another enormous boom. The Andy vibrated, spilling a box. It landed on the Captain's head, knocking him to the ground.

'Miles?'

'I'm already cycling the engines, Commander,' Miles said. 'There may be some slight discomfort while I...'

'Wyn, the Captain...' Hamza said.

'Do it. Everyone grab hold of something.'

Wyn dove for the ladder up to the flight module, clinging on. Miles fired the booster for two seconds. The ship felt like it was tearing itself apart. Miles cut the engine just before the point inertia inched the Andy upwards, defeating the moon's feeble gravity. The engines cut out, and the Andy slammed back down onto the ice, jolting Wyn's teeth inside her skull.

The Captain sprang back up to his feet. 'I said…'

'I took command given the urgency of the situation,' Wyn replied, as matter-of-factly as she could manage. She'd never seen fury in his eyes like now.

'Fine. I hope you haven't fucked our chances of getting off this rock,' Captain Davis said. 'Let's go.'

Wyn followed him out through the decontamination showers. Slowly, the air lock hissed and opened. They both jumped down, looking for signs of movement. The ice was clear, save for the smouldering carcass of the creature, at the edge of the booster's blast range.

'Careful,' Wyn said, as they approached the creature's smouldering husk.

It was dead. Its white eyes stared blankly forward. Half the body had burned away, leaving a mess of colourless entrails and red goo spilling across the ice. Wyn stepped forward and nudged it with her boot, to be sure. It was like kicking pudding.

'Zoe,' the Captain said. 'I think you'd better get down here.'

'Yes, sir.'

'Hamza, how are we coming on those weapons?'

'Working on it.'

'Work harder.'

Wyn scoured the horizon. 'If there were others, we must have scared them off,' she said. She looked at the Captain. 'I'm sorry about that,' she said.

'Forget it,' the Captain said. He sighed. 'Stef, Li, Ermine, do you read me?'

Nothing but static came back.

'They'll be okay,' Wyn said.

'What makes you say that?'

She shrugged. 'They have to be.'

He nodded. 'This is one ugly motherfucker,' he said, looking back down at the mess on the ice.

Wyn peered closer at the carcass, repulsed by what she saw. The gaping wound in the creature's side showed organs insulated by a thick hide of blubber. The fire burned it, spilling the intestines underneath. A closer look at its good side showed the creature had fins at its side, thin blades protruding from the end.

The creature's face made even its insides look pretty. The milky white eyes were barely even visible against the rest of its face. Clearly it had little use for them. The rest of the face looked vaguely like a walrus—its snout was large, with long white whiskers protruding—but instead of tusks it had two long, thin teeth, more like knives. Atop its head sat a dome of what would look like rock if it weren't so much apiece with the rest of its head. Hard, scratched, and thick, Wyn had no doubt this was what the creature used to try to take down the Andy.

It was the most ungainly, hideous looking creature Wyn could imagine, like a child had mixed up drawing its worst nightmares with a loveable sea creature, and made it come to life.

'Wow,' Zoe said, arriving on the scene replete with a box of implements, containers, and other medical apparatus. She gasped at the sight of the creature, but not in horror. If Wyn had to hazard a guess, she'd say Zoe was in love.

'Doc,' Captain Davis said. 'You work out what you need, take any samples you want, whatever it takes, okay? But foremost, I need to know how to kill it.'

'Boosters seem to do the trick,' Wyn said.

Captain Davis scanned the horizon. 'We still don't know if we had enough fuel to go for a hard burn the last time, let alone do it again,' he said. 'It's a last resort. It only works once they're at our... Shit.'

'What?'

'Over there. Hamza!'

'Coming.'

Hamza barrelled out of the airlock, box crate in his hands. He ran toward them.

Across the ice, on the edge of vision, more creatures appeared. One. No, five. Ten.

'What have we got?' Captain Davis asked.

'Bolt guns,' Hamza said.

'Bolt guns?'

'They'll fire a heavy-duty bolt a good fifty feet. They'll not take anything down at a distance, but they should do for close combat. I found four of them.'

'Okay. What else?'

'I modified two of the welders to work as flamethrowers, but I doubt they'll do much good. Li or Stef would be more use here, I'm afraid.'

'Anything else?'

'Unless you want the knives out of the mess?'

'Might not be the worst idea,' Wyn said. 'Captain...'

Creatures surrounded them, closing slowly in around them, too far away to be a threat, but close enough to see their white eyes.

Captain Davis pulled out a bolt gun. 'Go back inside, see if there's anything else you can work on.'

Hamza took a last look at the creatures and headed back inside, leaving Wyn and the Captain out on the ice, with Zoe knelt over the creature, making her examinations. The Captain handed Wyn a flame-thrower. It was clunky, long, and looked about as threatening as a garden rake. She pulled the trigger and a thin jet of flame arced lazily from the end, dripping burning fuel onto the ice.

'Let's see if that gives them pause,' she said.

'Not likely,' Zoe said, barely looking up from her examination. 'Their eyes probably register little more than vague shapes and colours at close quarters. As for heat, it'd be something so rare they probably wouldn't sense it as a danger, even if they could feel it through the blubber. Good news is it doesn't deal well with fire.'

'The bad news?' Captain Davis asked.

'This layer of body fat is pretty tough. I doubt one of those bolt guns would pierce the surface, even at point-blank range.'

'Head shots?' Wyn asked.

'Even worse. This whole top section to their head is harder than rock. It looks designed to cause some major damage. My guess is they use it to break up the ice, but it's hard to tell. It's about as hard as diamond, so your bolts would bounce off.'

'Shit,' Wyn replied.

'Yeah.'

'They're on the move,' Captain Davis said.

The creatures advanced with more pace, pulling themselves forward on their fronts with the claws on their fins.

'What do we do, Captain?'

'Let's get back on board,' the Captain replied.

'We might not get back off again.'

'One problem at a time.'

The creatures closed ground. They might not see for shit, but they sure as hell knew something new was on their ice.

A loud bark sounded from somewhere. A guttural, earthy sound. Wyn took it as a battle cry, and tightened her finger around the trigger, forcing herself not to close her eyes.

Instead, the creatures halted.

'What the fuck?' Wyn asked.

'Communication,' Zoe said, struggling to keep the level of unbridled excitement out of her voice. 'There's obviously a level of intelligence at play here.'

'Captain,' Hamza said over their headsets. 'I hate to add to the problems, but if we don't get back to the fissure soon, there's no way we'll be able to get under the ice before the magnetosphere crosses the threshold.'

Another bark. One or two of the creatures sniffed the ice.

As one, the creatures turned left. They looked to be in a hurry.

'They're leaving,' Zoe said. She almost sounded disappointed.

'Or they want a run up,' the Captain replied.

'Let's not look a gift horse in the mouth,' Wyn said, breaking the spell. The three of them stopped staring at the creatures and packed up Zoe's samples to take back inside.

'Fucking weird saying, if you ask me,' Hamza said, climbing down to help them. 'It was the people who didn't look in the gift horse's mouth who ended up getting killed in their sleep. If anything...'

A low, deep rumble cut him off. It started in their toes, building up through their legs. They each dropped their boxes, planting their feet more securely, holding their hands out to steady themselves. The rumble joined with a moan from the Andy's hull.

A crack rang out, like a thousand shotguns firing at once, so loud Wyn thought her head must be exploding. Forty feet away the ice split, right where an outcropping of ice rose a few feet in the air. The jut of ice grew by a dozen feet, juddering out of the ground.

A whooshing sound grew above the chaos.

'Get down!' the Captain shouted.

Wyn threw herself onto the ice.

A spray of water erupted from the crack, firing over a hundred feet into the air. Hundreds of gallons of water turning to ice in an instant before falling back down.

Toward them.

'Get under the ship,' Miles said calmly into Wyn's ear.

She got up and ran as shards of razor-sharp ice fell around her.

Interlude

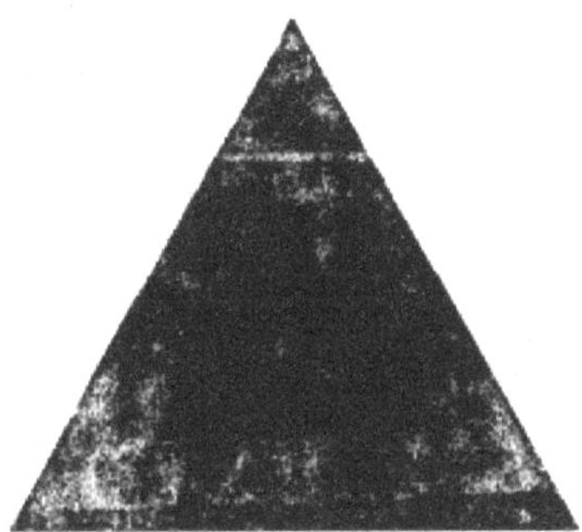

International Space Station – August 2107

'Focus on your landing,' Mary said, trying to force the concentration of her pupil. One of the nattering types, invariably the spawn of parents who indulged every whim and would probably offer a bribe when she failed their beautiful offspring.

'Sorry,' the boy said. 'Yeah, I kind of messed that up back there, didn't I? It's so hard to think when you're waiting to hear from so many schools and you're...'

She blanked the rest of it out. His idea of 'messing it up' was three missed turn signals, cutting up another person on the turn, and almost ramming a loader. Each one would be a fail in the pilot's basic, and he was two weeks away from taking that. He would fail. If she gave him a license, he was liable to kill himself or someone else. At least during their lessons he was in The Bug, a giant yellow beacon, easily seen and recognised by more experienced pilots as something to stay the hell away from.

Pass him and the little shit would be in some sleek black sports number, and be infinitely harder to avoid.

Out here, accidents meant death. It was that simple. But since the top universities across the globe decided a basic pilot's licence was a pre-requisite for entry to the elite level courses, her calendar was jammed not with people looking for actual pilot work, but with rich kids wanting something for their CV they would never actually use.

One attempted briber even put it that bluntly. 'Give my daughter a pass and I'll make sure she never sets foot in a cockpit ever again.' That particular father offered the equivalent of a year's wages. She still turned him down. It was only a matter of time before one of these rich kids caused a disaster. One of them reverses into the wrong part of the ISS, and the whole fucking thing goes down. Tens of thousands of people killed in an instant.

Not that anyone else seemed to care. Some hack gave the little simpering bimbo a pass, and since then Mary's revenues had been down about fifty percent. She didn't care. She'd kept her reputation, and if the bimbo killed anyone, it wouldn't be on her conscience.

She got rid of the talker, took the bug back to the hanger, and called it a day. Feeling exhausted, she needed a drink. She needed a drink a lot more nowadays, and while that worried her, it was in a 'wow I should worry about it at some point once I've had a glass of synth wine to relax,' kind of way.

'Mary,' a voice called out as she exited the hanger, heading into the main station. She turned to find Creeper running over. 'Wait up.'

Creeper was a pretty decent guy, but had a vague vibe of 'sex pest'. That he embraced the nickname to the extent nobody knew his actual name didn't help matters.

'What's up?' she asked, wanting nothing more than to turn her back on him and head straight to the bar.

'Your docking fee is overdue,' he said, giving her a look that he was sorry to be asking, but not so sorry he wouldn't give her berth away if she dicked him around.

'How much do I owe?'

'Seven fifty.'

She checked her wrist readout. Nine hundred. Sighing, she held it out to him. He scanned it with his own, and the number reset to one-fifty. Barely enough to get through to the end of the week. But if she couldn't berth, she couldn't earn. Sure, she could head out and park in the wilderness of black space beyond the station, but nobody took those teachers on. Especially not if they grew pesky things like morals and backbone.

'Thanks,' he said, turning away. She clocked him checking her chest out as he turned, and the look wasn't entirely complimentary. Bloody cheek of it. She checked one of the long mirrored glass fronts. Not so bad, she thought. She'd added a certain amount of curvature around her frame, there were wrinkles around her eyes, her hair starting to streak with grey. She still felt pretty good about the way she looked, though, more than most people could say at her age. Sure, her back looked like she'd escaped a dungeon, but she didn't care. She'd earned that scar.

She debated heading back to her bunk and changing before heading to the bar, but fuck it. She wasn't going there to meet people; she was going for a quick drink. Of course, those were the nights she ended up meeting someone. That wouldn't be so bad, either.

The Stumbling Juggler was the best bar on the ISS, the spaceport which outgrew its humble beginnings to become a permanent home for over a thousand people and a hub for thousands more. Mostly it was a way-station for those heading out to the moon bases, but with the recent introduction of the rival CSS, or Central Space Station, there was travel between them as well. Which meant a constant trail of people passing through. If she took a guy or a girl back to her bunk, she could feel reasonably certain she'd never see them again. Which made it pretty much perfect.

'Evening, Mary,' the barkeep—a young guy named Jin—called out. 'Usual?'

She nodded and headed over to her spot at the end of the bar. She was a creature of habit, and she liked the view here. Earth, endlessly screaming past the window at unfathomable speeds.

The view was getting worse, though. Even in the time she'd been up here, more and more green disappeared. Home was dying, and nobody seemed to have the slightest inclination to do anything about it.

Taking her glass, she took a little sip, saying a mental toast. Her little ritual at the start of a night.

To Alice.

Someone sat down a few seats along the bar, close enough to make conversation but not so close as to intrude. He flashed a smile. Vaguely familiar? Had she had a drink with him once? Hair thinning, bit of a belly, but the face seemed friendly enough. Not yet, but if he was still here in a few drinks time, maybe.

She took out her pad, a battered old piece of shit which didn't even update anymore. Not that she was bothered—it gave her the feeds she used. Who cared beyond that? She opened her socials, scrolled through for a second, before opening up a book. It would do until she got too tipsy to follow it.

'Excuse me,' a voice said silkily into her ear, making her jump. She turned, expecting the man from further along, but no. He remained engrossed in his own pad.

The silky voice belonged to a far-from-silky looking guy. Greasy hair plastered down over a pallid, sweaty-looking scalp. His suit ill-fitting, he was missing enough teeth to let you know his mouth was not a place you wanted to go near.

'Yes?' she replied, in a voice which made it clear she had no interest in the answer.

'Mary Kopera?'

She eyed him up again. How did this weaselling little shit know her name? 'Who's asking?'

He held out a sweaty palm. She stared at it as though it was a diseased lollipop. 'Andy Jones,' he said, smiling as though she should recognise the name. She didn't.

'And?'

'Here's your summons,' he said, dropping a piece of parchment on her lap. The smile disappeared. 'Consider yourself served.'

With that he was gone, leaving her stammering in her seat.

She opened the parchment and read.

It was exactly what she'd feared; the reason she was here. Her ex-husband.

Along the bar, a blonde woman approached the man at the bar, had a quick conversation with him, and dropped a parchment in his lap, too. He jumped up as though electrocuted. The blonde rushed away; her business done.

'You too, eh?' she said, waving her own summons.

'This can't be,' he said, staring at it. 'There's no jurisdiction here.'

'That's what I thought,' she said, frowning at her paper. She picked up her pad and checked the feeds. She never paid much attention to the local feeds for the station, but she looked now.

Chaos feared as station agrees extradition rights with planetary bodies, she read.

'Well, that won't be good,' she said, holding up the pad so her new friend could see it.

'Guys,' the bartender said, appearing from his little stall. 'Security alert across the station. I'm going to close up. Hope you don't mind.'

'Can we stay, Jin?' Mary asked.

'Sorry, hon,' he said.

'What's the problem?' the man asked.

'You're not from around here, are you?'

He shook his head. 'I'm running. From this.' He waved the paper. 'Not far enough, apparently.'

'Well, new boy, looks like your timing sucks.'

The ISS was one of the few places with no extradition treaties in place. Anyone wanting to escape the courts anywhere on Earth went to one of two places to hide out. Here, or if you were rich enough, the moon.

'Chickens are coming home to roost,' Mary said.

'Something like that. Judging by how quickly the process servers got here, I'd say we can expect a few police forces to be swimming around the station, trying to catch the fish who strayed out of reach,' Jin said.

'Fishes who don't want to be caught,' the other man said, a pensive look on his face. Mary wondered if he might be one of those fishes.

'Yeah, I don't think many of them will go quietly,' Mary said.

'Guys,' the bartender said. 'Seriously. I'd get to safety, and quick. I mean it.' He ushered them out and shuttered the bar.

The corridor was quiet. Shutters went down around the promenade, leaving a few confused shoppers and drinkers.

'Shit,' she said.

'What?'

'I left my drink in there.'

He smiled. 'If we get out of here, I'll buy you another one.'

She returned the smile. 'Are you saying that because you want to buy me a drink, or because you have no idea how to get to safety?'

'A bit of both?'

'Fair enough.'

A deep boom shook the walls, cutting the flirting off. She pointed down the corridor and started walking. She was still clutching the summons in her hands, so she folded it in half and stuffed it into her jacket pocket. Maybe she could claim it got lost in the confusion, ignore it completely.

'So, what's yours?' the guy asked. His own parchment had disappeared, maybe into his suit jacket. Nice jacket, too, she noticed. Out of the bar light, she could get a better look at him. Not overly handsome, but moneyed.

They moved through empty corridors until they came to the next port module. A hanger the size of an aircraft carrier, it held hundreds of docked ships, and hundreds of people clamouring to get onto them.

The way was most definitely blocked. As they stood at the top of the steps leading down, Mary could see no way through.

'Where are we headed?' the guy asked.

'Not this way, apparently,' she said. 'I'm a pilot. Only got a tiny Bug, but it'll be enough to get out of here until things calm down.'

'It's not in this bay?'

'Next one along.'

Another boom, closer this time, close enough to cause a panic in the crowd before them. Screams rang out, some fell to the ground. Somewhere in the morass, a fight broke out.

'Let's get out of here,' she said. Some in the crowd below were eyeing the ladder up, thinking of making a break for it. Mary didn't much fancy still being here when they did.

Heading back the way they came, Mary popped open the hatch of a trans-pipe, one of the maintenance ducts leading between the various 'spokes' of the ISS, with the original station entombed at their centre, unconnected and inaccessible, like a museum nobody could visit.

'You sure you know where you're going?' the man asked, crawling along the pipe behind her.

'A few months back some guy...' she started, but realised she didn't want to finish that particular story with a vaguely attractive man following her behind through an enclosed pipe. '... showed me a shortcut back to my dock.'

They made a sharp turn, heading downward, gravity shifting for the different sector. The Station controlled artificial gravity across the station in separate hubs so as not to place too much strain on the central one; it meant some weird tricks of physics when taking non-traditional routes about the place.

'Here we go,' she said, opening another hatch, which levelled them out and brought them into a corridor.

Straight into a riot.

A gigantic man knocked Mary to the ground almost instantly, watching what he ran from rather than what he was running toward. Armed police seemed to be the answer to both. Mary sprawled to the floor, the giant lunk of a man bouncing off the wall, getting back to his feet, and lumbering off.

Station security charged into the fray, bedecked in the latest riot suppressant kit coupled with space gear sturdy enough to survive exposure to space. The message was clear—mess with us, and we'll survive out in the vacuum a lot longer than you will.

'Shit,' her travelling companion said, pulling Mary backward. 'We need to get the hell out of here.'

She tended to agree, but as they turned to go, one cop raised his helmet and peered at the man stood next to her.

'You!' he shouted, starting toward both of them.

A door opened between them, and a stream of people fell out into the corridor, some holding bits of metal and plastic, most with their faces covered with cloth and bandanas. They got to their feet, roared like a collective animal, and charged the police.

His arm pulled on Mary's, and the two of them ran.

Alarms pealed at ear-shrieking volumes.

'Contamination alarms,' she shouted, breathlessly. 'A good excuse for them to depressurise the station, or chunks of it.'

'Best not be here when they do,' he replied, not looking back.

She struggled to keep up, despite the hand still clasped over her arm. Was he helping, or kidnapping? What the hell was going on, and who the hell was this guy? She didn't even have a name for him.

'Who are you?' she asked, hating the note of panic she heard in her own voice.

'Name's Char,' he replied, still not looking back. 'Where's your berth?'

'Straight ahead,' she said. People streamed past them, or stood around looking stupid, scared, or some combination of the two. She felt like asking for help, but felt silly even thinking of it. Hell, this guy wasn't so big; she could probably take him if she needed to.

So why hadn't she pulled her arm away?

She wrenched it free and stood her ground.

'I'm not going any further until you explain to me why the cop reacted like that?'

He stared back, confused. 'I thought he was looking at you. Honestly, I'm nobody. I want to get the hell out of here, same as you.'

She stared at her wrist, where deep red marks showed echoes of his grip.

'Come on,' she said.

Her dock wasn't used for commercial vessels, so there wasn't the mad crush they saw at the major terminal. Still, people rushed around, desperately trying to get off the station. Either running from the panic, or running from the cops. Probably both, in a lot of cases. What case was she? What case was he?

'Here,' she said, pointing to the yellow learner's bug sat in its mooring, uncoupled from the air dock. Someone had used it to get their own boat out. 'Help me with this.' She pointed to a lever.

Char grabbed hold of and levered it across the gap, while she tapped the mooring pad and started the docking sequence.

'This is your boat? You're a driving instructor?'

'That's me,' she said.

'At least we should be safe, out there.'

'That's the theory.'

The mooring coupled, she opened the hatch, smelling the stale air of the bug's interior as it wafted past her into the hanger. She needed to give it a good clean.

They climbed in, Mary going first, Char closing the hatch behind her.

'What's the range on this thing?' he asked.

'We could feasibly make it back to Earth, if that's what you're asking.'

'That's not the plan?'

'This'll take a few hours. A day at the most. We've got enough life support for two of us for up to a week. Let it die down and head home. Sounds like a plan to me.'

'Home to you,' he said, in a low voice.

'You're welcome to find another ship if you want to head back to Earth,' she said, getting testy.

He held his hands up in surrender. 'I'm entirely at your mercy,' he said.

'Strap in there,' she said, pointing to the co-pilot seat from which she usually gave instruction, taking the hot seat for herself. She disengaged the clamps, logged a request to leave with the docking authority, who didn't even acknowledge it.

She reversed out, turning to face space as she went.

'Woah,' he said, as the planet below faced them through a wide pane of glass.

A jetliner, engines revving wildly, pulled out in front of her, cutting off her route. It picked up speed, and if it completed its pass before she got out of the way, its heat vents would likely melt them in their seats. 'Hold on,' she said, pushing the bug into a hard dive.

She may not be pretty, but the bug was a great little ship, tiny and nimble. Both became instant blessings. The dive into what should have been empty space found instead two Interpol gunships. Darting left, she manoeuvred round both, pulling sharply up.

The sky was full of ships, each desperately trying to get off the station, each behaving erratically. If this were a flying test, pretty much every pilot would fail. Mega-cruisers, yachts, other bugs, light and heavy class freighters, they darted around each other with no rhyme or reason.

It wouldn't take long before they started hitting each other, she thought, and no sooner had the thought left her subconscious than it came true. A rich man's yacht, probably driven by the kind of idiot she'd flunked, banked too hard at something still over a mile away. It crashed right into a freighter, the spear of its elegant design puncturing the tank, igniting an explosion which enveloped both ships.

If there was panic in the skies, it doubled instantly. Collective insanity took hold, and ships crashed into each other left and right.

The heat from one blast charred their windshield, flames licking across the glass and leaving soot marks before the vacuum of space snuffed it out.

Mary twisted and turned, this way and that. Retching sounds came from the passenger seat, and she hoped vaguely her cockpit wasn't about to fill with globules of zero gravity vomit. Then something else ran right across her flight path, and she had to react.

She had no idea how long it took before some sense of calm returned to the surrounding skies, but by the time it had, they'd drifted far from the ISS itself. Between them and home was a field of debris and bodies. Ships incapacitated, ships destroyed. It was like sitting at the edge of a battlefield.

'Good driving,' Char said. She looked over at him—he'd turned a shade of puce she'd never seen on a person before.

'Thanks,' she said. 'We're not home and safe yet.'

It was true. Some ships drifted back toward the planet below, but navigating anything in this mess was like playing with a loaded gun. Not only that, but the debris was likely to get caught in a different orbit and slingshot around them at thousands of kilometres a minute. That made the ISS a sitting duck. It made them one, too.

'What do we do now?' Char asked.

'We wait,' she said, unbuckling from her seat. 'Tell me if you see anything scary.'

'Where are you going?'

'Drink,' she said.

The back of the bug had a tiny cabin where she kept her most prized possessions, not trusting the security of the station. Chief of these was a small urn, sat inside a locked box under the chair.

Also inside was a food and drink printer, which she was glad to have restocked in the last week. Who knew how long they'd be out here?

Hunger seemed a long way off. Her system was too flooded with adrenaline for that, but coffee sounded good. She poured two cups and headed back through. She handed one to Char, who took it gratefully.

'It's shit, but it's like rocket fuel.'

'As long as it's hot,' he concurred. He smiled at her. 'You saved my life. Thank you.'

'It's nice to have the company while we wait.'

They sat in silence and watched the debris. Mary's eyes couldn't help but go to each body floating past them, damaged beyond recognition by the elements of space, compressed and pulled almost to breaking point. Eyes imploded, lungs misting around their mouths like a haze. It wasn't the first time she'd seen it—hazards of a life above the sky—but this was something else.

'I wonder what's going on back at the station,' Char said eventually.

'Not going to be pretty.'

'I imagine not.'

'A lot of criminals on there. Not many will go quietly. I don't know what possessed them to make the treaty.'

Char nodded and stared ahead.

Why would the Earth's only Free Port sign up to an extradition treaty? The International Space Agency had long maintained it couldn't show preference to any nation state. Of course, illicit kidnappings had happened there for years. There was no official extradition treaty, but there was no sovereign state to claim asylum to, either, so you hid at your own risk, since there was nothing to stop any nation sending its people to make a snatch.

Most of the criminals on the station weren't master criminals; far from it. People avoiding summons or waiting for heat to die down on their latest job, mostly. There were minor cartels, and more sex pests than you could shake a stick at, but nothing to justify this chaos.

So what had changed?

Must have been someone pretty damn important.

Someone recently arrived.

She sipped her coffee. 'So,' she said. 'What was your summons?'

He laughed. 'Unpaid parking tickets.'

'Really?'

'Sure. Yours?'

'Bastard ex. He wasn't happy with what I took from him. I needed to get away. Figured he'd not chase me this far.'

'Guess he did.'

'Guess so.' She watched as three ships converged together. Interpol ships, by the looks of them. Scouring the skies, looking for someone. 'So, I told you the truth. What say you tell me yours?'

She looked over at him. He flashed a smile. 'You figure something out?'

'Getting a whiff of it.'

He reached inside his jacket, pulling out a stem gun, the kind of weapon smugglers and thieves used. Long, slender, made of biodegradable plastic. It left no prints, was undetectable, and if you saw one, it meant you were about to die. 'You've got excellent senses.'

'You bastard.'

'Sorry, love,' he said. 'I needed to get out of there, and I saw the pilot badge on your shirt.'

She looked down. She still had her work top on. Idiot.

'What was your summons?' she asked.

'Honestly, there's so many people out there after me, I'm amazed it was the first one to find me. Like I said, it was unpaid parking tickets. The least of my many problems.'

'And the most?'

'That'll be the charge of international genocide.'

Her blood froze, and her stomach churned.

'You're Charles De Witt?'

'One and the same.'

She looked him over, nausea rising in her chest.

In the wake of the great floods in Britain, millions fled the northern cities of Liverpool and Manchester. Heading inland to the Pennines, they became stranded on a range of hills offering protection but no means of survival. Cut off from the south, the British government—or what remained of it after the flooding of the capital—wondered what to do with them. De Witt was a General in the Army, one with a novel idea. He bombed the hills, killing over a million people. Called it 'putting them out of their misery'. Once the condemnations rolled in, he disappeared, evading capture ever since.

Out of the viewscreen, three Interpol ships kept heading toward them.

'Well,' she said. 'Looks like they've found you.'

'Looks like it.' He took out the parking ticket summons and looked at it, giving a wry smile. 'Tracer,' he said, crumpling it up and throwing it behind him. 'Of course. Not stupid, this Interpol lot.'

'What are you going to do?' she asked, trying to ignore the rising bile at being in such a confined space with a true monster.

'I'm sure you'd like me to say I'm going to hand myself over. I'm afraid the answer's no.'

As the docking request came in from the lead Interpol ship, she hit accept, flipping the screen straight off. 'Oh, really?'

He raised the gun to her face, the charming facade gone. 'What have you done?' he asked, calmly.

'I've accepted a docking request from Interpol and disengaged the bug's console. They have us in traction. Nothing can stop it, because the console is hard-coded to accept my instruction alone. So we're clear, I'm not going to give it, no matter what you do. You evil motherfucker.'

'We'll see.' He lowered the pistol and shot her leg. The bang reverberated around the tiny bug like a cascading roar.

She screamed and clutched her leg. Blood oozed from the wound, floating up through her fingers in the Zero-G atmosphere.

'Turn it back on.'

She took her jacket off and wrapped it around the wound, fixing him with a steely stare.

'Fine,' she said. 'But I need you to get me something, since you shot me in the leg. Back there.' She motioned to the tiny bunk. 'There's a locked box.'

He eyed her, distrustfully, and unclipped his buckle.

She watched, tears welling in her eyes, as the Interpol ships closed the distance. Not long.

He brought out the wooden box.

'Open it,' she said.

He tucked the weapon into his jacket and set the box down. He opened the top. It freed the tiny wooden urn, which floated up into the space between them.

'That's Alice,' she said, wincing through the pain. 'That's the reason my ex-husband is after me. I stole her, you see.'

A dark look passed over De Witt's face as he realised what was in his hands.

'You killed my daughter, Mr De Witt. Your bombs. My husband and I barely escaped with our lives. We were the lucky ones, out on the edge of the camps. If you can call us lucky. I have scar tissue covering my back, from your bombs. I saw such terrible things.'

The dawning realisation that he was out of options didn't come close to remorse, but it was enough. She didn't want his remorse. She wanted to rip his face off, to stamp on his bones until they were as close to ash as what was in the urn he held.

'We carried little Alice's body for miles, swapping her between us, until we came to a town. We never could get over her death. The only thing we couldn't split between us was her. So I'll be damned if I'm going to give you any opportunity to escape. You are going to answer for your crimes, you malicious, evil fuck.'

De Witt slumped back in his chair, his face ashen.

The docking clamps gave a deep boom as the Interpol ships took the bug and held it firm.

De Witt fished out his weapon, staring at it as he considered his options.

She was out of her chair even as he turned the weapon on himself.

She snatched it from him, swinging her fist round, connecting hard with his jaw.

'You don't get away that easy,' she said.

The dock opened. Interpol officers streamed through, rushing their prisoner, who'd begun moaning like a stuck pig.

She grabbed the urn as it floated past her, gathering it close to her chest.

She could take it home now.

She was ready.

Chapter Five

Lois fought against the darkness even as it threatened to envelop her, spat blood onto the ground and pushed herself up, noting the various cuts and bruises littering her body. Pain seemed to swallow her whole.

Above her, sirens sounded. Nobody had been foolish enough to follow her over the edge. They'd be coming, though. It wasn't hard to back up and come down the hill.

Her clothes hung tattered and torn, strips of them soaked in her own blood. A quick examination of her face with her fingers found more than one source. Fuck. If she had any chance of getting through this, she'd need to melt into the city's residents. Difficult when you look like you've fallen down a mountain.

Slowly, willing each of her limbs back into motion, she started forward. She slipped off her shoes, one of which had lost a heel somewhere along the way, and ran.

Her best bet was to get to Findlay's apartment. He'd know what to do; he had evacuation protocols. All being well, he already had the chip she'd left in her door frame.

Unless Sunset had the chip.

Stumbling forward, she tried to walk as casually as possible. This was the commercial part of town, but the residential quarters were not far away. Sunset had severely rebuilt Atlanta once they bought it wholesale; they lay it out exactly as a committee of HR representatives would. A city with no life or soul to it, but rigid lines of delineation.

Findlay lived in the section of town designated for those in service to Sunset—those running restaurants, cleaning apartments, working in the schools, the hospitals. Much more than half the city's population, an ecosystem of their own in some regards, but nobody was under any illusions—they were there to service Sunset. Or to serve those who served. Most of these worked for Sunset subsidiaries—Sunset had every contract for miles around sewn up. Schools. Hospitals. Hell, even the vets were Sunset subsidiaries.

Nobody could get an apartment unless they could show their worth to the community, and nobody who worked in this half of the city could cross over to the other side without a Sunset employee ID. It was economic segregation, but that didn't make it much different to other cities across America. Just more efficient.

Lois ducked down an alleyway between buildings, wary of the coverage of the network of floating eyes in the sky. She'd need to stay out of their sight if she could.

Lois may have lived here for a few years, but she didn't know the city well. Findlay had told her where his temporary apartment was, but only in reference to its location being on her pod circuit journey to Sunset. The pod rail was fifty stories up, so it was a pretty useless reference frame.

She tried to get her breath back, get her bearings. Hover pods traversed the sky. She couldn't see them, but could hear them. No doubt looking for her, along with the eyes. She found a window and checked her reflection. It wasn't good. She wiped the blood from her face, dumped her jacket, and tried to damp down her wild hair. Still, she looked like she'd walked away from a car wreck.

The bustle of people sounded a few blocks away. Heading toward the sound, she found herself on a wide open street she'd never seen before. To each side, huge shops several stories high stretched out. She must be near the invisible divide between the two cities.

People stared aghast, moving out of her way with such haste they collided with each other. Lowering her gaze, she focused on the shiny sidewalk, its electroglass panels glinting in the morning sun.

She ducked into a clothes shop, grabbed at a few comfortable clothes, and mumbled something to the gawping shop assistant about the changing room. The assistant pointed vaguely toward the back of the store. Lois took a handful of different clothes toward the back, ignoring the increasingly persistent calls of 'Miss? Miss?'

Diving into the changing room, she closed the door and peeled her ruined business suit off, wincing as rough fabric moved over open wounds. She'd need a visit to a pharma, too. Pulling on the new clothes, she found they didn't fit, but they were the only option. She'd need some comfortable sneakers, too.

The urge to sit in the changing room and black out threatened to overwhelm her, so she pulled the tags off the clothes, ran them through the scanner on the wall, and held her wrist up to the scanner to make the sale.

Declined, the message on the screen said, in diminutive but hostile lettering. Scan invalid.

She tried again and got the same response. What the fuck? These chips were supposedly regulated from a vault somewhere in fucking Utah. Unhackable. How the hell had Sunset rendered her a non-person within, what, half an hour? Not to mention she was a government employee with access protected beyond the means of a standard citizen. She'd expected monitoring, not erasure.

She sat back down. Without a wrist scan, she wouldn't be able to get into buildings, pay for food, contact her family.

Findlay. She had to get to Findlay.

She barged out of the dressing room, leaving her ruined clothes in a heap, trying to walk with the authority of someone who has nothing to fear.

'Miss,' the tall store security guard said, standing directly in her way, thick arms crossed in front of him.

She couldn't think what else to do but to shove him, which she did with as much of a run up as her knees allowed. It wasn't pretty, but it got the job done. She may be half his size, but off balance he fell like lumber, almost getting enough grip on her new loose-fitting clothes to pull her down with him.

The man who'd pointed her to the changing room stood terrified. She ignored him, heading right for the door. She grabbed some shades on the way out, putting them on and merging into the heavy flow of pedestrians in the street. Feed shades were a kind of halfway house for those who couldn't afford the Oc, or were unwilling to have one bolted onto their optic nerve. Her field of vision filled with ads for toothpaste and debt management services, as well as news of her escape. They were a cheap model, ad supported. Practically useless. The local feed, itself a part of Sunset's entertainment and information division, described her as an escaped terrorist responsible for the murder of a resident on the south side of Atlanta.

She stopped, trying to get her bearings. The shades tried to sync with her wrist implant, but couldn't. So, the implant wasn't just blocked for transitions, but cut off from the feed entirely. Perhaps she'd damaged it during the fall, but her wrist was one of the few parts not currently crying out for medical attention, so it seemed unlikely.

She'd have to get rid of it, somehow.

Findlay. He could do that.

People crushed around. Not Sunset people, but they bore the horror of instant recognition. She was already famous.

Shit.

It was hardly surprising. Out on the street—underneath signs for a local Pentecostal church and ads for chemically enhanced orgasm aids—a billboard picture of her, taken this morning, inside her pod. Scowling, looking mean.

People hustled to get out of her way as reports came through on the feed of sightings in the area—considered armed and dangerous; already assaulted one person in her attempt to flee justice. Streets away, sirens sounded.

She threw the shades to the ground—useful as they may be, they confused her brain. The constant scrawl of feed info was too much, one of many reasons she'd not gone in for the Oc craze of a few years back. She looked up to the pod rail above, trying to get a sense of where she was.

North. She needed to head north.

Moving as quickly as she could without running, she kept on. She didn't want to give herself away even more. Besides, her left knee seemed intent on stopping any attempts at speed. Moving off the main streets meant fewer people and less recognition. At least one busybody probably called the cops already.

The cops. If she couldn't get to Findlay's, was going to them such a bad idea? No, Sunset would have them locked down too.

Four streets down, some measure of recognition tickled the back of her brain. She looked up to the pod rail above again.

This was it.

Findlay's place. At least, somewhere up there was.

A man came out the building, and Lois moved quickly to the door, placing her foot in the way to stop it closing before easing her way inside.

The central atrium was large, dusty, and empty. With no chip, there'd be no way of using the elevator unless she caught a ride with someone. Also, the risk of recognition while locked in a confined little room was too great. No, she'd have to take the stairs.

Fuck.

She didn't even know which floor Findlay was on, but each hallway had a window. If she went up until she could see the pod rail, that would be it. In theory.

Lois dashed up the first twenty floors with an urgency that matched her predicament and belied the pain in her legs, but beyond that her tired and battered body decided it didn't want to climb any more stairs, thank you very much. The rest of the climb was like pulling herself up a mountain using an invisible rope. Sweat made her stolen clothes cling to her back, and she remembered halfway up she'd neglected to get sneaks up to the task—roughly around the time her soles bled so much they made her feet slip.

In the end, she didn't need the window to tell her she'd reached the right floor. It was clear from the police tape, the soldiers waiting in the hallway, and the sight of Findlay's body, his throat cut from ear to ear as he lay across the threshold to his apartment.

Chapter Six

For the next few weeks, Judd didn't get to leave Walker's small flat. He didn't get to see many people, either. Mr Walker, Mrs Smith, and Lan were the extent of it, each spending a few hours a day with him. They used Walker's study as a classroom, working with Judd to test the extents of his powers, teaching him the basics of how their gifts worked, demonstrating their own talents, and generally being cagey about what their end game for him was.

'One thing I must impress upon you,' Walker said one afternoon as Judd contemplated how long it had been since he'd been outside—years stuck inside on the moon and as soon as he was back on Earth he got ushered into an old man's flat—'Is we do not use our gifts on one another.'

This was far from the first time Walker had impressed this upon Judd. In fact, he'd done so half an hour earlier, while Judd wondered idly where the old man was living since Judd took up residence in his home.

'Sure,' Judd replied, 'so I don't get to use my gifts, since the only thing they seem to be good for is blocking off other teeps?'

'I wouldn't say that,' Walker replied, leaning back in his chair. 'We're talking to each other in our heads, right now.'

'You're the only one I can do it with. Anyway, aren't we using our gifts on one another? I'm beaming my thoughts into your head, and vice versa. Doesn't that count? Or do the rules only apply to what I can do?'

'The rule extends to malicious incursions into the brain. It covers TK's too, preventing them from using the force of other objects against their fellow gifted.'

'Answer me a question,' Judd asked, out loud this time. He still found talking inside his head disconcerting. 'If you're governed by the same rules, how the hell did you find me, and how did you get me down here?'

Walker smiled. 'You've been thinking about this a lot, haven't you?' he said, joining him in out-loud conversation, his real voice far weaker.

'I have a lot of time on my hands these days.'

'You think I scanned you from Earth, came up to the station and planted thoughts in your mind? That I pulled you away against your will?'

'You telling me you couldn't?'

'Except for scanning you from Earth, yes. But no. Let me tell you what actually happened. Your parents, they're from Ohio, right?'

'Dayton, yeah.'

'What did they do for a living?'

'Both civil servants. Worked local government.'

'Sure. Dad away a lot?'

'Sometimes.'

'Would it surprise you to know he was one of us?'

'Dad?' The image of a robust man in drab clothing rose to the forefront of his mind. Thick moustache smelling vaguely of sandalwood when Judd kissed his cheek. 'Honestly, I don't know. I was so young when he left.'

'Your mother never knew. Part of the code is we don't tell our children until they reach an age where the gift can present. Back in those days it never used to present until late teens, so it was never an issue. Your father, well, let's say he left the flock.'

'What, so, because my Dad had the gift, you flew to the moon to see if I did?'

'The fact you'd never presented symptoms made you low priority. When I came to see you, I wrote you off as a norm until your voice rang clear in my head. You weren't even aware you'd done it.'

Judd's stomach turned at the thought of it. 'I remember.'

'As for planting thoughts in your head, I don't do that to our people. As soon as you started talking to me, inside, I let things run their course. I have to admit, I didn't think your talents would shake out to much, given how long you'd lived in darkness, but there you are. We are nothing if not a consistently surprising breed.'

Judd took Walker's words in. They had the ring of truth about them, but how did he know the old man wasn't still messing with his head?

'How do you like my apartment?' Walker asked.

'It's fine,' Judd said. 'I can't help but think it should be you in it, not me.'

Walker waved a hand, dismissively. 'I'm fine. Plenty of places to lay my head. At my age I'm not one for sleeping, anyway.'

'Why am I not in one of them, letting an old man sleep in his own bed?'

'Why do you ask questions you already know the answers to?'

Judd shook his head. 'I'm in here because you don't trust me. You think I might melt people's heads.'

Walker scoffed. 'You think that's why you're in here?'

'Sure.'

'Oh, Judd. I'm afraid the truth is much worse than that,' he said, with a half smile to soften the blow. It turned to a frown. 'The people in this facility despise you. Are terrified of you. There are powerful gifted in this facility, more powerful than me. To them you are a threat. They would gladly wipe your mind, leave you in a coma, or squeeze the blood vessels around your brain stem rather than see you walking around. You wiped the gift from one of them. In a hundred years of this gift, nobody has ever done anything like it.'

Judd stared at the table, fighting back the anger. 'I'm never going to leave this room?'

'Quite the contrary. Once we've decided you're in control of your powers, we will introduce you to the others. In due course. You forget I have a lot of sway here. The fact Mrs Smith and I are protecting you has kept you safe, for the time being. When we tell people you're not a threat, things will be different.'

'And if it doesn't happen?'

'It will.'

There was a knock at the door.

'Ah,' Walker said, moving his chair back from his desk. 'Lan's going to work with you on the geometry of telekinesis, I believe?'

Judd nodded. He didn't much feel like learning anything else today. He didn't much feel like spending time with Lan either. She clearly resented him, kept their sessions as brief and work-manlike as she could. The door opened, and Walker made his excuses, leaving him alone with Lan. He watched her, though she never looked up at him. To think he thought he might have a chance with her—she loathed him, was terrified of him.

'So,' Lan said, in clipped tones. 'Shall we start?'

Judd nodded, his attention already drifting elsewhere, to thoughts of teeps in the corridors, firing mind bullets at him.

Chapter Seven

Lois stared at the body of her handler. Her friend. Her only way out of this mess.

Findlay's body took the count up to three Interpol agents with their throats cut, plus a civilian. Each killed with the brazen hallmark of someone enjoying their work. This was the work of an individual, backed up by the might of the world's most powerful organisation. Whoever did this likely had her in their sights and knew exactly where she was.

Those crowding around the body looked like local PD rather than Sunset security, but given the white overalls it was hard to tell. Could be the person who'd cut Findlay's throat stood before her, cataloguing a scene of their own making. Either way, there was no point trying to get in for a closer look, or to flash her Interpol credentials around for the local PD. For one thing, she didn't have any.

There was no sign of Detectives Jones or Stone on the scene. Nothing resembling a friendly face. She had to get out of there.

Easing back into the stairwell, the enormity of Findlay's death hit. She'd long considered him a friend, because he'd done his job with quiet authority, asked about her life, her kids, and done everything he could to address her concerns, deflecting talk of himself. Now he was dead. And she didn't know a thing about him. He'd saved her life, more than once, and the one time she could have returned the favour, she was too late.

Findlay was her tether to Interpol. She wouldn't even know where to begin to reach out to his superiors. Panic rising up the small of her back, she picked up her pace down the stairs. She had to get out. Get out of the city. Get to her girls.

Turning a corner wrapped in thoughts of her next move, she forgot to pay attention to what was coming the other way. The soldier coming up the stairs was as surprised as she was. They clattered into each other before tumbling down, Lois somehow staying on top of the soldier, whose cries of pain suggested he had the raw end of the deal.

'She's here, in the stairwell,' he cried.

Sunset.

Doors opened, soldiers pouring into the stairwell above and below. The soldier underneath her tried to land a punch but missed, hitting her shoulder. Lois tried to hit back, but her connection with the soldier's jaw made little impact, and the second attempt hit the side of his helmet. Pain shot up her arm. She followed up with two more punches, ineffectual paws that at least forced him to block them. She wrestled his gun off him, dropping it on the steps so it clattered away, and scrambled to her feet.

Shadows moved in the stairwell above and below. Lois barged through the door to the nearest hallway, limping badly from some knock she'd taken on the way down, knee protesting at every step. She expected it to be full of more soldiers, but it was blissfully empty, save for a cleaning droid which took no notice of her. Running down the long corridor, she passed a sign alternating instructions for evacuation with political ads. She waited for the proclamations in favour of the re-election of the incumbent Mayor to end, and the evacuation routes to come back. Beyond the far door, footsteps sounded as soldiers convened.

It was a fire escape, but there, too footsteps sounded on the metal. Lois's heart sank at the realisation she was trapped. The only ways out were the fire escape and the stairwell, both teeming with soldiers.

She could let them take her. She was an agent of the government, which should provide some small measure of safety. But the image of Findlay's dead stare came to mind. They weren't interested in what she had to say, and they sure as hell didn't fear the government. They feared nothing. Whatever she had stumbled across on that pad, it was enough to commit murder most brazen.

The apartment doors were solid anti-burglary carbon, like every other door in this city; she turned and kicked at the nearest one on the off-chance. After a few kicks, her knee protested more than the door did.

She turned to the far end of the corridor. The soldiers shuffled beyond the door. Getting themselves into the optimal position to attack. She tried to recall what little combat training Interpol had given her and planted her feet in a fighting stance. She'd have no chance, of course, but she'd go down swinging, if nothing else.

A gun sounded in the stairwell beyond the door, a single shot, but it jolted her out of her position.

The door burst open as a soldier flew backwards through it, a burst of red flying up from his helmet as he fell, skidding along the ground with a howl of pain. Lois glimpsed the man's assailant in the doorway, little more than a silhouette, before it flooded with more soldiers, obscuring her view.

The door closed once more before bursting open again, and the attacker pushed two more soldiers through it into the corridor. They didn't fall back, but faced up against their assailant, guns drawn. The assailant, clad in their own black tactical gear, whipped up their own weapon, aiming it at the first soldier.

'Put the gun down,' the soldier said, his voice far from commanding.

'You first,' the figure opposite said, her voice far surer of itself.

Lois moved up the corridor while the two soldiers had their attention away from her. The first fallen soldier stirred. Lois reached down and took his weapon. Stepping toward the action, she pressed the barrel to the base of the second soldier's skull. 'Better do what she says.'

Both soldiers raised their hands, letting their guns go limp. The woman in black moved forward, gun still trained on the soldiers, and took their guns. With a flash of movement, she brought down the butt of one onto the first soldier's nose, breaking it and sending him to his knees in a howl, before spinning round and kicking the second soldier in the chest.

'Come on,' she said, before Lois could even register what was going on. 'There'll be more.'

The woman dashed back out the door, Lois trailing behind her into a stairwell covered in dead and unconscious soldiers.

Her saviour said nothing on the way down the stairs, which she took at a speed Lois struggled to keep up with. She stripped off her tactical gear as she descended, gathering it under her arm in an oddly graceful movement. A stocky woman, shorter than she'd seemed in her armour, with dark hair tied back in a bob. Lois couldn't get a good look at her face from behind, too busy trying to ignore the pain in her knee to try.

At the bottom of the stairwell, the woman ducked under the stairs and pulled out a black holdall, from which she took out a black wig, shades, and a cap, thrusting the bundle to Lois to put on, along with some shoes. She stowed her tactical equipment in the bag, gathered it over her shoulder, and put on her own cap and glasses.

'Let's go,' she said.

'Wait,' Lois said, adjusting the wig and putting the shades on.

The woman didn't wait, heading for the doorway, hat pulled down low to shield her face from the eyes in the street. Lois adopted the same pose, keeping her gaze fixed on the sidewalk in front of her and the retreating boots of her new friend. She looked up enough to see a battalion of reinforcements offloading in front of the apartment building. They ignored the two women leaving together and poured into the building.

With Lois following behind they walked in silence, her new friend not stopping for breath or pause, Lois trying to keep the limp out of her walk as much as possible. They moved in and out of crowds, through back alleyways, through shops where security guards watched them intently, and back out onto the street. Lois was lost instantly, though she was sure they hadn't moved far from their starting position.

The other woman ducked into a building and headed straight for the elevator.

The elevator ride was silent despite their being alone. The woman kept her head down, so Lois did the same. When the doors opened once more, they headed out into the corridor which bustled with people coming in and out of the doors, dressed in various uniforms of service staff, laughing and joking with each other. None paid attention to the two women moving through them to the last door. Her friend waved her wrist over the scanner and headed straight into the apartment. Lois followed, pulling the door closed behind her.

The woman pulled off her hat, and the black bob, revealing close cropped red hair beneath.

'Detective Stone?' Lois said.

Stone turned to Lois and wordlessly crossed the room, grabbing her by the throat. She had Lois up against the door before she could react, her hand pressing down hard on Lois's windpipe.

'Okay, Blondie. You mind telling me who the fuck you are, and why I had to rescue you?'

Chapter Eight

Diving under the safety of the boosters, Wyn cowered as shards of ice ricocheted off the hull with an almighty clatter.

A scream pierced the din. Zoe lay prostrate on the ice, howling and clutching her leg as ice showered down around her.

Captain Davis was the first to react, using the low gravity to propel himself across the ice. Wyn rushed out from under the relative safety of the Andy to help. Captain Davis scooped up the biologist, who swore with such Australian profuseness it almost distracted from the jutting shard of ice sticking out of her knee. Together Wyn and the Captain brought her back to the relative safety offered by the booster's shadow.

'Open the doors,' the Captain bellowed.

Wyn ran to the doors, hitting the button.

The geyser stopped, and the sounds of ice hitting metal subsided. Wyn could make out other shattering sounds and prayed they weren't coming from her flight module.

Water gushed across the surface, freezing over before it reached them.

'Back inside!' Captain Davis shouted.

'No!' Zoe shouted. 'You put me through the decontamination showers, it could kill me.'

'She's right,' Barnes said, appearing through the showers himself, suited up and carrying a med kit. 'Lay her down on the ground.'

They lay Zoe down, her body convulsing with shivers the moment she became still.

'Shit,' Barnes said. 'Miles, how's her suit integrity holding up?'

'There is a sizeable tear in the right leg of her suit, but currently the ice, as well as some blood flow, is sealing it, preventing the...'

'Okay, good.' He looked at the shard. 'Shit.'

'What do you need?' Captain Davis asked.

'Not to be on an ice moon,' Barnes replied. 'If I take her in through the decontamination showers, the chemicals will get into her bloodstream through the ice, and kill her. If I remove the ice and try to patch it, she will die.'

'So turn off the showers,' Wyn said.

'No!' Zoe cried out.

Wyn ignored her and ran to the Andy. She went through the burst of decontaminating water and into the cargo bay. She ran to the decontamination showers and pulled the unit connecting it to the ship's power. 'Bring her in!' she shouted.

Barnes and the Captain carried the limp biologist through the showers, laying her down on the ground before heading back outside. Wyn connected the shower back up, and the two of them came back through. Wyn closed the doors, re-pressurising the cargo bay.

'Hamza?' she called out.

'Up here,' Hamza said, descending from the ladders up to the main deck.

'Any damage?'

'Not that Miles or I can see. Atmosphere is holding, for now.'

'Help me get her suit off,' Barnes called. He was on his knees, leaning over Zoe. 'Wyn, get me an oxygen bag.'

'Don't mean to add complications,' Hamza said. 'But we need to leave.'

'What are you talking about?' Barnes said.

'If we don't head back to the fissure, we won't make it back before the magnetotail crosses the horizon, and we die. We have to leave.'

'He's right,' Zoe coughed, her head free of the helmet, a shocking blue spreading around the corners of her mouth. 'Go. The mission is more important than I am.'

'Zoe, without you there is no mission,' Wyn said.

Captain Davis stepped forward to Barnes. 'Doc, can you stabilise her to take the trip?'

Barnes shook his head. 'If I don't remove the ice, and we go out there, the cold will kill her in about five minutes. It's fifty-fifty whether she gets hypothermia in here. These suits protect us against temperatures of minus two hundred degrees, but the shard sticking out of her will be like a conduit right to her nervous system.'

'So take it out,' the Captain replied.

'I can't. The ice has fused with her flesh. If I pull it out, I could pull whole tendons out, not to mention the arteries already severed.'

'Can you save her? Honestly.'

'Yes. But I need an hour. If I can bring the temperature up slowly, I can remove the ice, make sure there's no damage, and close the wound. Maybe two hours?'

Captain Davis shook his head. 'Doesn't leave us long, Doc.'

'You three head off,' Barnes said. 'Take the tracker. We'll be behind you. Wait as long as you can.'

The Captain stood, staring back down at Zoe.

'Captain, without Zoe, there is no mission.'

'Okay,' the Captain said. 'Hamza, Wyn, you're with me. Doc, you get back as quick as you can, right?'

'I'm staying with them,' Wyn said, before she'd had the chance to think it through. 'We'll move a lot quicker with two of us, and I can patch Zoe's suit while the doc is working.'

'Are you sure?'

Wyn nodded. 'If we don't make it, you can handle the drive home.'

'I'll do my best.' He grasped Wyn by the shoulder. 'Make it, yeah?'

They put their helmets back on, Zoe, Wyn and Barnes included, to allow the others to leave. As soon as they were gone, Wyn took Zoe's helmet back off. The biologist had tears in her eyes.

'You should have gone,' she said.

Wyn shrugged. 'Let's get this suit fixed.'

Barnes worked on Zoe's leg for an hour, easing the ice away from her flesh until he could remove it. A spurt of arterial blood followed, but Barnes reached into the wound and grabbed the disparate parts of the artery.

Wyn looked away, taking a torch to Zoe's suit to patch up the tear. It was frightening how easily a shard of ice had punctured through what was supposed to be the most resilient space suit ever made. The material—fabric woven with an alloy with a name longer than a Russian novel—was designed to withstand unbearable extremes in temperature and radiation near the levels generated by the Minos's nuclear engines. It was not designed, however, to be a suit of armour. Wyn thought about those creatures, their teeth, those claws, and she shuddered. One of those would make quick work of these suits.

By the time she looked again, Zoe's leg was patched up.

'You'll struggle to walk properly,' Barnes said, bringing Zoe back round from the meds he'd used to calm her. 'The ice severed an artery, and took a chunk of your calf muscle, too. You'll be on crutches for a while. Or you would be, if we had any. For now, I've dosed the shit out of you with painkillers.'

'Thanks,' Zoe replied, a hazy smile on her face.

'Good work,' Wyn said, bringing Zoe her suit.

'Thanks,' Barnes replied. 'You too.'

'Oh yeah, I'm a wiz with an acetylene torch.'

'No, I mean with the Captain. On my own I would have lost that argument.'

'Captain would have seen sense.'

'If you say so. Anyway, let's get out of here.'

They sat Zoe up and helped her back into her suit.

'I think I'm going to throw up,' Zoe said.

'If you're going to do it, do it before we get your helmet on.'

Zoe nodded, but didn't spew.

'How are we going to do this?' Wyn asked. 'We've got no transport, and she can't walk.'

'Did they leave us any weapons?' Barnes asked.

Wyn looked around. 'One bolt gun, one flame thrower.'

'Okay. I'll carry Zoe. You take the weapons. I guess we walk.'

'And if those things attack?'

'We'll be easy pickings and die a slow, gruesome, and no doubt extremely painful death.'

'Right.'

Wyn picked up the flamethrower and opened the airlock. As the doors pulled across, she half expected to see a line of the creatures waiting, but there was nothing but ice as far as she could see. 'Come on,' she said, reaching back in and taking Zoe's arm under her own. Barnes took the other, and the three of them clumsily exited the Andy.

'Wait,' Wyn said, once they were on the ice. She ran back and grabbed a pad from the side. 'Computer,' she said. 'Plot a course to the others.'

'Yes, Commander,' came the ship's computer's stilted voice.

Back outside, the light had faded. Jupiter no longer filled the sky, and they couldn't see much more than a hundred feet in front of them. Wyn closed the cargo bay doors, noting the creeping red working its way up the metal support struts.

'Miles?'

'Yes, commander?'

'How long until the magnetotail threshold?'

'One hour and thirty-seven minutes.'

'And how far away are the others?'

'Two point seven kilometres.'

Barnes huffed. 'Well, we'd better get a move on.'

'Miles, you keep an eye on the Andy, yeah?' Wyn said, feeling a pang of loss at the thought she might not hear from him again until this was over.

'I don't have eyes, Commander.'

'I can never tell if he's being obtuse, or sarcastic,' Barnes said.

'A little of both,' Wyn replied, straining with Zoe's weight, even in the low gravity. Whatever cocktail Barnes had given her, it was doing its job—she lolled between them, scarcely attempting to move forward under her own volition.

At first, they made good progress, Wyn watching the pad to make sure they headed in the right direction. A countdown clock ticked down in the pad's corner, its inexorable decline to the threshold matching the hammering in Wyn's heart.

They moved forward in silence, Wyn contemplating what would happen if the magnetotail crested the horizon. Wyn's head filled with images of flesh boiling, eyes exploding in her skull. Things drilled into her at school as though the personal apocalypse she'd encountered in London wasn't enough for one lifetime.

She pushed the thought down, focusing on putting one boot down on the ice after another, and keeping Zoe beside her. They should be able to see the others, she thought, looking at her pad.

They'd crossed well over two-thirds of the distance, and not in bad time, so she'd expect to at least see the twinkle of lights ahead.

'I need a minute,' Barnes said, puffing.

'We can't stop,' Wyn replied.

'Please,' Barnes said. 'A minute. I need a minute.'

They stopped and lay Zoe down on the ice. Barnes scanned her suit with his own pad. Wyn checked her own.

'Miles?' she called.

There was no answer.

'Captain Davis?'

No answer.

'Radio's been kerfluey since we got here,' Barnes said, still puffing away.

'I know,' Wyn said, frowning at her pad once more. 'But we should be close enough to raise the others.'

'Hey, Miles,' Barnes said. 'Captain. Ermine. Li. Stef. Anyone reading this?'

Silence once more.

Wyn was sure they'd come the right way. It was the ship's computer who'd sent them this way, after all. Hell, she'd seen the indentations in the ice from the Tracker.

She looked down at the ice. No trails.

They were lost.

'Anyone?' she said, fear strangling her voice.

'What's going on?' Barnes asked, getting back to his feet.

'We're on our own,' Wyn said.

She stared at the sky. She was a navigator, and what did good navigators do when they got lost at sea? They looked to the heavens.

Except these weren't her heavens.

'What do we do?' Barnes asked, sounding a lot like she felt.

'Shh a second,' she said. She held her hands up to the sky, doing calculations in her head.

Jupiter was there, and the sun is between... We're tidally locked, so that would mean we're...

She screwed up her face, trying to squeeze every ounce of brain power out. 'Give me your pad,' she said.

'It's configured to be a medical scanner,' he said, handing it over.

'Thanks,' she said. Tapping on the home screen, she went into the root menu, trying to find the single scratch pad she could mark down the maths in her head; drawing her finger in long arcs over the screen, scribbling the numbers down so chaotically the pad couldn't even translate them. She was so engrossed, she nearly missed the blinking message notification.

COMM%NDER.

She clicked on it.

PROT0COLS OVERWRITTEN.

Wyn called up the keyboard to respond.

Miles?

YES.

What the hell is going on?

\TTEMPT TO KEeP ZOE FROM CONTINU*7g MIS-SION.*

What?

CANNOT SdY MORE>>

HURRRY**

The chat screen closed, taking Wyn back to her scrawled calculations. At lightning speed, they solved themselves, Miles doing the work until the path was clear.

HUR^Y

The screen showed their path, and their place on it. They were a mile away, with twenty-three minutes to get there.

'I've got it,' Wyn said.

'Um, Commander?' Barnes said.

Wyn looked up. Surrounding them in a wide circle at the edge of their own light, a wall of the creatures stood, raised up on their hindquarters, silently appraising the three humans before them.

Chapter Nine

'What do you mean, who the fuck am I?' Lois asked, as forcefully as she could through a windpipe half closed off by the detective's grip. 'You had me in interrogation for hours last night.'

Stone let her go, dropping Lois to the floor, gasping for breath. The redhead paced around the small room. 'Six months of deep cover, and I've got to drop everything to go rescue some middle-aged business bimbo from a fucking army. I need to get my fucking head examined, going along with this.'

'Undercover?' Lois asked. 'Undercover with whom?'

The redhead stared at her with a look hard enough to melt steel beams, but said nothing.

'Look,' Lois said, getting to her feet. 'I'm undercover, too. Interpol. Working inside Sunset. My cover got blown. In a big way.'

The look softened to something approaching hesitant curiosity. 'Must have been, the way Secure went after you. They don't normally send an army after one person. You must have been close to something.'

Lois shrugged. 'They got me before I could find much out. What's your deal?'

'No deal. Working, same as you.'

'Well, if it weren't for you, I'd be dead, or in a windowless torture dungeon, so thanks. I'm Lois.'

She held her hand out. The other woman looked at it, hanging there in the air, but didn't take it.

'Katrina,' she said, finally. 'But call me Kat.'

Lois withdrew her hand. 'Okay, Kat. What do we do?'

'Us? I don't know about you, but I'm done. One handler down already. Now this. Get you out of there, that's all I knew. I'm going to go back to my new handler and see what's what. Hopefully, it'll be me getting the fuck out of this shitty city.'

'What about me?'

'You're on your own, Princess.'

Lois leaned against the wall, exhausted.

Kat disappeared off into another room. Lois heard the frantic sound of someone throwing their entire life into a bag.

First things first. She needed to get hold of Marisa, make sure she was safe. The thought she might not be formed a knot in her stomach.

'Do you have a phone I can use?'

'No phones,' Kat snapped back. 'Nothing traceable. Do you have a mask on your wrist?'

'I, uh...'

'Jesus wept. Come on, I'll take you to my handler, he'll sort you out.'

'Sure,' Lois said. A state of numbness crept over her, which meant going into shock, shutting down. She couldn't afford it, but seemed powerless to stop it. Tiredness crashed over her like a wave.

'Hope this Findlay guy is more reliable than my last handler,' Kat half muttered.

'Wait,' Lois said, snapping back to the present. 'Findlay? That's who I was going to see. His apartment.'

'What?' Kat said. That was enough to halt her mad dash to cram her entire life into a single holdall.

'He's dead,' Lois said.

Kat started packing again, with even more gusto. 'Fuck. So, you got him killed. Two dead handlers in as many weeks. Christ, I need to get the hell out of this city.'

'No,' Lois spluttered. 'Look, will you fucking stop moving for one second? We're on the same side here. We need to talk. Work this out?'

'No,' Kat said. 'We need to get the hell out of here.' As if to prove her point, sirens sounded not far away from the window. Kat crossed to the blinds and peered down. 'Shit. They're here.'

'Fine,' Lois said. 'We've got to go. But we should stick together.'

'Whatever,' Kat said, throwing her bag over her shoulder. 'Put your hair and cap back on and try to keep up. You fall behind, you're on your own.'

She threw open her door and left. Lois grabbed her disguise and followed.

Keeping up took more effort than Lois expected. Even with the heavy holdall swung over her shoulder, Kat was a nimble escapee, fast on her feet, giving Lois little in the way of clues as to the twists and turns they were to take. Lois started out a few feet ahead of her, a distance that tripled by the time they left the building, and tripled again by the time they reached the end of the block.

They walked past the patrol pods pulled up outside Kat's building, the attention of the police officers and soldiers on the front doors rather than the side exit they had taken. Lois followed Kat's lead and didn't give them a second glance, pulling her hat down and focusing on the street. Up ahead, Kat ducked down an alley. Lois followed, but Kat was out of sight by the time she got there. Lois paused, looking around until she saw her once again, on the far side of the adjacent street.

How the fuck did she do that?

If Lois was going to keep up, she'd have to run, which would draw too much attention. She resumed her brisk walk, trying desperately to keep Kat in her sights, so much so she nearly walked straight into a patrolling police officer, ducking left at the last moment as he thankfully looked right. But she'd lost Kat once more.

Shit.

Carrying on up the street, she was on her own once more. Following the footsteps of an obviously skilled agent, she'd felt secure, as though in some kind of safety net. Now anyone could be an enemy; every glance might be a way of tracking her down.

She stopped, struck dumb in the middle of the street.

'You going to stand there like an idiot?' Kat said behind her.

Lois span round. Kat leaned in a doorway, smirking.

'Come on,' she said. 'I wanted to test you.' She started moving again, but at a pace Lois could match.

'Test me?'

'I figured if you're setting me up, you'd have the skills to keep up. Guess you're not playing me.'

With their exit taking place at a more manageable pace, they cleared the centre of the city. Kat said little except to guide Lois, who stuck to her side. Nobody gave the pair a second glance—people getting on with their lives, most of them with the vacant stare of Oc wearers, their attention barely in the present at the best of times.

The primary worry was an Oc scanning their faces and alerting Sunset to where they were, so they kept their caps low and their gaze lower. The feeds they saw in cafes and shops showed Lois's face, but not Kat's, so nobody paying attention would look for two women. That suited them fine.

Kat headed up the stone steps of a townhouse which had seen better days and keyed a code into the call-box. The door opened, and the two of them moved inside.

'We should be safe in here,' Kat said. 'I doubt they'll know about this place.'

'What is it?'

'A safe house. Not the agency. Goes back beyond that.'

'Back where?'

'The League.'

Lois stopped. 'The League?'

'That's what I said.' She dumped the bag down and moved through the house. Lois followed.

Great. She'd moved from outcast to terrorist by association. The League. The thought alone was enough to send a shiver down her spine.

Dust lay thick over every surface. Nobody had been inside these walls for years—decades, even, but Kat still moved methodically from room to room to be sure. 'We're clear,' she said once they reached the top of the house. 'Let's see what we've got to drink, and we'll get that wrist scanner masked.'

They headed back down to the small kitchen, Lois thinking that anything surviving in there would be well beyond its best. Kat opened a cupboard and plucked out a bottle of old whisky. 'This'll do,' she said, pulling two dusty old tumblers out of a cupboard. She rinsed them in a sink, the old pipes rattling and groaning through years of disuse. Even after rinsing, Lois eyed them with suspicion, but Kat didn't ask permission. She poured two healthy glasses and slid one across the old worn plastic table top.

'To Findlay,' she said, picking up her drink and downing it in one go. Lois picked hers up and did the same, keeping a picture of Findlay in her head. Him stumbling into her table at the restaurant a few nights ago. Had that been the moment which sealed their fate? Had the restaurant owner been the one to tip them off? Or had it been in Sunset's view the whole time, waiting for confirmation?

She needed the chip. It was the only leverage she had. But she had no idea whether it was still stuck in the doorjamb of her house or if Findlay had picked it up. Either way, it was somewhere they couldn't go.

'You okay there?' Kat asked, pouring herself a second glass of the whiskey.

'Thinking,' Lois replied. 'Trying to work out how we got here.'

'We're not going anywhere tonight. Might as well try to work it out together.' She picked up her tumbler and moved through to the sitting room.

Lois poured another glass and followed her through, bringing the bottle.

'So,' Kat said, easing herself into a sofa so old it creaked under her. 'I'm guessing you didn't tell the whole story down at the station. You want to tell me what the fuck is going on?' She fished out a box from under the table as she asked, pulling out a set of nasty and rusty looking tools. She motioned for Lois's arm.

Lois joined her and held her wrist out, looking away as Kat got to work. 'I'm in Interpol's deep cover corporate crime unit,' Lois said, trying to ignore the scratching sensation on her wrist. 'My wife and family live here, and after Sardy and his handler got killed, I got parachuted in from another assignment to try to find out what got him killed, and by who.'

'You have family here?'

'I got them out yesterday.'

'Good.'

'What about you?'

Kat blew out a hefty sigh. 'Been inside the Police Department here for six months. Trying to get the skinny on the links between

Sunset and the force. I've also been on the trail of Sardy and Jones's killer. Or killers.'

'You knew them?'

'Jones was my handler. I never met Sardy. She recruited me about, shit, seven years ago. I was ex-League. She gave me the chance to...' She stared at the glass, turning it in her hands.

'To Jones. And to Sardy,' Lois said.

They clinked glasses and drank once more.

'You and Sardy must have found some troubling shit,' Kat said.

'I wish I did,' Lois replied. 'I got access to a rack pad, given to me by the head of security herself, and had less than a day to look through it before they turned on me. Findlay gave me a capture lens and a chip to log everything. I got one day's worth clocked, and I don't even know where the chip is. Fuck.'

'So we don't have leverage?'

Lois shrugged. 'Sorry. Does this place have a comms line?'

'What for?'

'My wife and kids. I need to make sure they're okay.'

She shook her head. 'No comms. This place is a dark spot. No ether, no web. Nothing. Only way to be sure they're not snooping. Sorry.'

Lois nodded. A dread crept over her. Whatever came next, she'd have to make sure her girls were safe.

The story continues with
BLACK CLOUD

Grab the next thrilling installment of the
SUNSET CHRONICLES

SCAN ME

Leave a review

I really hope you've enjoyed reading Blinded by Light.

If you did, the nicest thing you could do for me right now is to leave a review. Reviews are absolutely crucial to discoverability, and social proof. If you could take a second to rate and review this at the store of your choice, I'd hugely appreciate it.

Thanks,

Paul

Author's note

One part of launching a monthly serial that's great fun is that I've ended up with a load of new covers to design. I got really into digital art and cover design a few years ago when I redid the covers to my Blood on the Motorway series, and I'd say I almost spend as much time these days in Photoshop as I do in Scrivener. So I won't pretend that part of the decision to split 9 books into 45 wasn't partly informed by a curiosity as to what I could do with a canvas that big.

I find it pretty helpful in terms of procrastination avoidance to have two completely different artistic addictions. If I procrastinate over my word count, for example, I can open up a cover design and pootle about on it and not feel like I'm working, because I'm not doing the thing I'm supposed to be doing. But since I'm still making something, the time isn't as lost as if I, say, spend the time doomscrolling.

When I thought of the Sunset Chronicles as a serial, I had to have a think about the covers I wanted to make for them. The glorious thing about writing serialised fiction is that it's designed to be like a bag of popcorn; consumable, disposable. It's like the old pulp novels which had so much serialisation in them, anyway. So I really liked the idea of making covers that evoked that old style. Weather-beaten, worn paperbacks, like picking out an old classic at a used bookstore or car boot sale. Except, these are futuristic books, set a hundred years in the future.

There are elements of everything from alien horror to cyberpunk dystopia in there, alongside more traditional sci-fi elements and old-school thriller and murder mystery elements. And they are (for the moment) digital only. So how the hell do you try to convey that in a cover?

I decided to find out...

The first thing I made was a standard template which includes a series logo, and a header that tells people exactly where they are in the series. You'll see it at the top of every book in the series, so when you're flicking through your e-reader, it's really easy to keep track of where you are.

SUNSET CHRONICLES

Obviously, there are nods in the design here to horror books of the 1980s, and this kind of design has also been used more recently on a Netflix show that shall not be named. But this design style is kind of exactly where I want the series to be. I want to invoke the nostalgia of how reading books as a young man made me feel, but then look beyond that.

Once I had the series iconography, I set about playing. I now have nearly a dozen of these covers in various states of completion, but the first four covers are now out in the wild. Five now, if you count the 'keep reading' page a few clicks back. (You can actually preorder/order Black Cloud right now if you click on the link)

Each one conveys a distinct element of the first series. Each one complements the episode itself, but is also (I hope) a cool little keepsake of its own, something that'll look great on your digital bookshelf. I've dedicated this episode to a writer's group I'm in called Writers United, which remains one of the most gloriously happenstance writing group ever to form online. We met many years ago when we all submitted to the same national writing competition — the organisers completely failed to get in touch with anyone for months on end, and we all met slagging them off on a Facebook thread. Thus was a glorious friendship born. None of us won the competition, but the array of talent in the group is a source of constant inspiration to me.

I really hope you're enjoying the series so far. As I write this, I'm putting the finishing touches to the second season, so there's plenty of road ahead.

Happy reading,
Paul

JOIN THE HOLLOW STONE

Join my reader's group
and be the first on the planet
to hear about new releases,
and get exclusive content
you won't find anywhere else.

SCAN ME

GOT BLOOD?

An apocalyptic storm. A killer on the loose.
The battle for humanity's survival starts here.

SCAN ME

About the Author

Paul Stephenson writes pulp fiction for the digital age. His first novel series – the apocalyptic *Blood on the Motorway* trilogy – has been an Amazon bestseller on both sides of the Atlantic. A former journalist, he has a diploma in Creative Writing from Oxford University.

His stories have been featured on the chart-topping horror podcasts, *The Other Stories* and *The Night's End*. His newest project, the ebook serial *The Sunset Chronicles*, is a dystopian sci-fi thriller that will delight and terrify fans of science fiction and horror alike. He is also the creator of the podcast *Bleakwood*, tales of terror from a mysterious English town, and one half of the *All Creatives Now* team, with fellow horror author, Kev Harrison.

He lives in England with his wife, two children, and one hellhound.

To keep up to date with his books, please visit his website PaulStephensonBooks.com

Also by Paul Stephenson

DARKNESS RISES

When darkness comes, it doesn't ask permission. Get Darkness Come Alive, the first book in the new vampire epic from the author of Blood on the Motorway and the Sunset Chronicles.

BLOOD ON THE MOTORWAY

Blood on the Motorway
An apocalyptic storm. A killer on the loose. The battle for humanity's survival starts here.
Sleepwalk City

The fight for control has begun. Who will prevail in the battle for humanity's future in the pulse-quickening sequel to Blood on the Motorway?

A Final Storm

The sky is full of lights once more, and the survivors will need more than luck to get them through the coming storm. Who will survive, and who will thrive, in this heart-pounding finale to the Blood on the Motorway saga?

SUNSET CHRONICLES

Plague. Murder. Unrest. Humanity's future looks far from bright.

The year is 2107, and Earth is dying. For Wyn, Lois, and Judd, that's the least of their problems. Each holds a key to Earth's cure and humanity's survival in The Sunset Chronicles, the new sci-fi horror thrill-ride from Paul Stephenson, author of the bestselling British horror saga, Blood on the Motorway.

BLEAKWOOD

Introducing Bleakwood, a horror podcast from the creator of Blood on the Motorway and the Sunset Chronicles.

In the years since the fall, many of us have tried to find out why. To find what lead us here. But with so much of the old world gone, there are more questions than answers. What tore a hole in the world? Can we ever get it back?

But I think I've found something. A binder in the rubble. Don't ask me where. Full of stories about a little town called Bleakwood, stories that seem to show a way that....

They're not in any order, really. And I might be wrong. They might not have the answer. But I think it's in here.

A way back. To the before.

Listen, I'm just going to read them out, and you judge for yourself.

DARE YOU VENTURE INTO BLEAKWOOD?

WHAT TORE A HOLE IN THE WORLD?
CAN WE EVER GET IT BACK?

Find out in Bleakwood, the new horror podcast from the creator of Blood on the Motorway and The Sunset Chronicles

Created and narrated by Paul Stephenson and with stories by some of the most exciting voices in British modern Horror, subscribe to Bleakwood for a fresh story every month.

SCAN ME

www.ingramcontent.com/pod-product-compliance
Lightning Source LLC
Chambersburg PA
CBHW010440170726
48283CB00011B/3306